# THE YOGINI

## PRAISE FOR *THE YOGINI*

'In case you thought that Sangeeta Bandyopadhyay needed one more show of excellence to cement herself as one of the great feminist writers of today, *The Yogini* is it. It's a novel which makes use of creeping, unsettling, surrealist horror to create an atmosphere which reflects the real lives of women today who are shackled by the things they cannot control'—Will Harris, Books and Bao

'*The Yogini* constantly challenges the reader, sometimes in following the twists it takes, but more intensely in the problems it asks you to share with Homi. This effect is enforced by the editorial note on niyati that opens the novel'—Daniel Lubin, Savage Online

'Bandyopadhyay slowly dismantles the trappings of the conventional novel as Homi experiences what can only be described as a spiritual crisis which will lead us to an ending far from the romcom echoes of the opening. (. . .) That this remains only one possible interpretation suggests the pleasurable complexity of this wonderful author'—Grant Rintoul, 1st Reading

'In *The Yogini*, I also saw influences of authors like Angela Carter in the juxtaposition of the grotesque alongside the ordinary. But, surpassing these comparisons to western counterparts, Bandyopadhyay's writing shines through in this excellent translation as unique and exciting. Exploring themes of female identity and sexuality in a rapidly modernising and changing India, *The Yogini* is unlike anything else I've read in a long time'—Yasmine Rose Reads

PRAISE FOR *ABANDON*

'*Abandon* is a bold, important and formidable novel about the demands of life and the responsibilities we have, both to others and to ourselves'—Lucy Scholes, *National*

'Audacious . . . The need to create, Bandyopadhyay suggests, is something like a permanent wound—inextricable, smarting with pain, and only denied for so long'—Darren Huang, *Words without Borders*

'A compelling novel about the perpetual conflict between art and life'—Rabeea Saleem, Book Riot

'Tragic and beguiling'—Callum McAllister, *Cardiff Review*

'All through the book, a strange author-voice—in that responsible tone people adopt when enjoying the delivery of bad news—reminds you again and again that what you are reading is fiction. But when I finished that author voice's book, after watching the 'I' watch its own characters burn, I felt abandoned. Since then, I have been trying to work out how to catch up'—Caleb Klaces, *White Review*

'Breathtaking and urgent; exploring women's desire and struggle for creative, economic, and sexual independent in Bandyopadhyay's characteristically sensual and engrossing prose, *Abandon* is an absolute joy'—Megan Bradbury, author of *Everyone is Watching*

'In this beautiful novel, which subtly examines the rift that can open up inside us, compassion and cruelty are so close that at times they become indistinguishable. Prepare to be wrenched apart'—Rowan Hisayo Buchanan, author of *Harmless Like You*

# the YOGINI

## Sangeeta Bandyopadhyay

Translated by
ARUNAVA SINHA

PENGUIN

An imprint of Penguin Random House

HAMISH HAMILTON

USA | Canada | UK | Ireland | Australia
New Zealand | India | South Africa | China

Hamish Hamilton is part of the Penguin Random House group of companies
whose addresses can be found at global.penguinrandomhouse.com

Published by Penguin Random House India Pvt. Ltd
7th Floor, Infinity Tower C, DLF Cyber City,
Gurgaon 122 002, Haryana, India

Penguin
Random House
India

First published in Bengali as *Jogini* by Ananda Publishers 2008
Published in the United Kingdom by Tilted Axis Press 2019
Translation funded by Arts Council England
This edition published in Hamish Hamilton by Penguin Random
House India 2019

ISBN 9780670093533

For sale in the Indian Subcontinent only

Typeset by Simon Collinson
Printed at Thomson Press India Ltd, New Delhi

www.penguin.co.in

MIX
Paper
FSC  FSC® C010615

# THE YOGINI

# Niyati

---

At the heart of *The Yogini* is the idea of fate,
'niyoti' in the original Bangla. It might be simple
to interpret fate (the word used in this translation
instead of destiny, which, as Tilted Axis founder
Deborah Smith pointed out, is now a Disneyfied
term) as the opposite of free will when it comes to
the existence of the individual.

In India, though, niyoti – or niyati in Sanskrit – can
be unpacked to mean a lot more. The etymology
provides a literal meaning of being led or carried,
which can of course be interpreted as an absence of
agency – the anguish about which drives this novel.

But in some aspects of Shaivite philosophy – the
description of the ascetic in the novel makes him
resemble the Hindu god Shiva in some forms –
niyati also refers to a state in which the individual
is under the illusion of being bound to a particular
time and space, when in fact they are not. So, in
its earthly manifestation for human beings, niyoti/
niyati is a constraining factor for the individual but
still not real, only illusory.

## RETURNED TO HER SENSES
## FOR THE FIRST TIME

It was late into the inflated night when she returned to her senses for the first time. She found herself standing by the door of a train compartment, holding the handles and swaying with the train as it hurtled along. Her body lurched alarmingly from side to side. She was leaning forward perilously. She would fall out of the train at any moment.

Was it time, then? she wondered. Was this how she and her fate were to be separated? Was this, finally, what fate had written for her?

The tracks seemed to howl fiercely at her when she looked down. Sparks flew from the friction of steel against steel. All she had to do was loosen her hold for everything to end.

Rattling a thousand chains, her soul cried out, Freedom! Freedom!

And she decided to jump. But then someone

gripped her elbow. She didn't turn around. There was no need to, for she knew who it was. She could see the hand clamped on her arm – the wrist encircled by rosary beads. A copper band, an iron chain, a red thread, chunky amulets. He scavenged for all sorts of things to slip around his wrist. Mounds of grime were gathered beneath his long nails. She raised her eyes to look – not behind her, but ahead. There was no beginning, no end, only a train passing through an endless expanse. No artificial lights shone now – the world beyond was lit generously by the moon, its beams crystallised in pools of water in the fields, the light magnified a million times by the reflections. The train raced through a silvery kingdom. Her heart was disproportionately heavy – but she no longer had cause to be sad or angry.

An icy current whispered in her ear, 'Homi! Homi! Empress?'

'Come closer, Empress.'

How much closer, man with the matted locks? Haven't I already given you the right to claim me? So many thoughts flow through my head, but not one of them will lead to anything tangible. Not one will leave a physical imprint on the planet. Such notions, only some of which I embrace. I let go of the rest, to ensure that you have no power over me – neither over the causes of things happening to me, nor over their effects. Not even over the merging of cause and effect, because both are mechanical in my life, just as you are, an automaton. This is my final observation about existence. There is no such thing as free will here. No fundamental independence. I have long accepted that I have a natural fate in this world, a human being's fate. I am no one, fate is everything. You are everything. This way, I can be closer to you too, can't I?

These thoughts ran through her head, but she wished, too, to escape, to be free. A strange force took hold of her. She jerked her arm out of his grasp, and, the very next moment, whirled around to strike at the figure with the matted locks. With all her strength she lashed out at him, hoping that the impact would throw him off the train.

## THE PAST: CHAPTER ONE

Homi heard Sulagno and Rajatkanti talking on her way to the conference room. They were field reporters, and were discussing some sort of tragedy. 'This is fate, Rajat-da,' Sulagno said, 'what else can you call it?'

Rajat was yet to light the cigarette clamped between his lips.

'We don't know what fate is,' he said. 'Sometimes it all seems to be coincidence – and then at other times it feels like all occurrences are merely a set of tools, the instruments used to ensure that what is pre-destined actually happens.'

Instead of continuing on her way, Homi walked back towards them to ask what had provoked this corridor discussion about fate when they should have been busy preparing for their prime time bulletin. She found herself surprised by their conversation, as though she had never before heard that word: fate.

'What's all this about, Sulagno?' she asked.

'The case of the lift operator, haven't you heard?'

Homi shook her head. She hadn't heard anything. She'd been so busy wrapping up her 9:30 segment that she hadn't even had time to take a coffee break.

'This old lift in a Padmapukur building, you know, it was stuck between the third and fourth floors. The lift operator managed to get the door open and help eight people to safety. And then, would you believe it, the cable snapped or something and the lift dropped all the way to the ground floor like a stone in a well. He couldn't get out. Head smashed to pieces.'

'You went to cover it?' asked Homi.

Sulagno nodded with a forlorn smile.

'It shocks you?'

'No, I'm just wondering why he couldn't get out. All the others did. The rescue mission went on for nearly seventy minutes, everyone else was saved, except him. Why? The cable stayed firm the whole time they were moving around inside the lift, their combined weight could have made it snap. And then, just as the last person was about to escape...'

'Fate,' said Rajatkanti.

'You're right, it was fate. He was destined to die that way.'

Homi felt physically ill as she listened to them. Her stomach churned.

'What are you saying?' she said. 'Fate? What's that, Sulagno? Do either of you really think such things have a role to play in our lives?'

Sulagno looked at her.

'They do. Beyond a doubt they do. I know it's ultimately fate that drives us, and nothing else. You can do what you like, but really, you're nothing more than a fish caught in a net.'

Rajatkanti's phone was ringing.

'What are you looking so heartbroken for, Homi? Your fate will drag you to Park Street very soon – bet on it.'

'Are you partying tonight?' Sulagno interrupted.

'No,' said Rajatkanti, walking away. 'I'd have told you if we were.'

Homi continued towards the conference room, where Yash Vaidya was waiting to hold the last meeting of the day.

## THE PAST: CHAPTER TWO

Several days had passed, and the brief discussion about fate had slipped from Homi's mind, which was entirely natural. While any incident instantly turned into news on this 24-7 TV channel, unceremoniously bursting in on viewers, it wasn't long before the ripples of excitement died down, some other newsworthy event competing for viewers' attention by then. These occurrences often raised deep ethical questions in the reporters' minds, even causing distress at times, but everyone had to throw themselves at whatever news was breaking the very next minute. There was never any time to absorb what happened – incidents took place, the bulletin was made and presented, analysed and debated, but you couldn't stop there.

'Can you tell me the difference between literature and news?' the CEO of the media company had asked Homi when interviewing her three years ago. Perhaps he had posed this particular question because she was a literature student. Homi had not had to grope for an answer.

'If news is the rain, literature is the water that gathers underground,' she'd replied. 'The rainwater falls on the earth and seeps slowly through each of the layers underground before eventually becoming pure. News is what happened a moment ago – it has to pass through layers of time before it can become literature. When time and philosophy are added to news, what you get is literature.'

Rishi Patel, the CEO, had stared at her for half a minute. Homi remembered him telling her they would talk more about this when they could find the time.

But she didn't remember how many days had passed since the conversation in the corridor. She'd left the office around 10 PM and was attempting to cross the busy main road when she saw a hermit standing directly opposite, impassive in a haze of light cast on the pavement by Jimmy's Kitchen, the Chinese restaurant. Even from a distance it had seemed to Homi that his piercing gaze was trained on her. But she had to look away before she could register what was happening. He was gone by the time she crossed the road. Curiosity piqued, Homi went up to the entrance to Jimmy's Kitchen and looked for him. Was it possible she'd made a mistake, that there hadn't been anyone there at all?

A mistake? But his sharp, terrifying glance had embedded itself in her consciousness in an instant. She had felt a distinct stab of fear. At that moment someone whispered to her from her left, very close by.

'Empress?'

Goosebumps prickling her skin, Homi turned to look at him. A chill coursed through her veins. Bitingly cold.

He looked fearsome, his matted locks and beard framing his face like a spider. His eyes blazed, and his body gave off a mild stench. She thought it could be marijuana.

Homi recoiled.

'Who are you? What do you want?' she wanted to say. It was possible that an unimaginable fear kept her from uttering the words.

'Don't you recognise me, Empress?' He adjusted the blanket draped haphazardly around his shoulders.

Again, she retreated as he approached her, holding out a hand with tongs in it. A hermit's usual paraphernalia. It was obvious no one else could see him, since it was impossible for such a frightening man to advance towards a lone woman, especially at this hour of the night, without anyone intervening.

She realised quickly that she wasn't able to seek help from any of her colleagues, many of whom were milling about on the opposite pavement. She would have to deal with this man all by herself.

Coming to a halt, she asked in Hindi, 'What do you want?'

The hermit brought the two arms of his tongs together repeatedly, making a series of clicks. His tall, lean frame stiffened, and Homi saw obsession and desire come to life in his glowing eyes.

'Come closer.'

A cruel but frantic voice. Barbaric diction.

The man signalled to her again.

'Come. Come closer.' He made an obscene gesture.

'You don't recognise me, Empress,' he said after a brief silence.

'I am your fate,' he continued – and disappeared at once.

## THE KISS AND
## THE LONG SHADOW

This was the first time fate had sunk its claws into Homi's life. She hadn't been alert to its presence – had never had the chance to be on her guard. A gigantic oil tanker was pounding down AJC Bose Road. Getting quickly out of its way, Homi reflected on what fate was, and how it might be defined. She didn't know. None of her experiences so far had appeared pre-destined. She had always considered every incident a means for adding to her experiences, experiences that helped her understand herself better, that answered fundamental questions – who am I, what am I, why am I? – to assemble the distinct, solitary individual to be signified by the word 'I'.

But although the man with the matted locks had evaporated into thin air, the word 'fate' hung in the air around her, a cloud of melancholic mockery closing in on her relentlessly. She seemed to have shifted into a different world, where the ground beneath her feet had loosened and left her feeling exposed.

Is he my fate? Homi asked herself. Suddenly she wanted to vomit. Her body felt violated, desiring numbness, as though it had assumed all this time that she could never have been subject to fate. Never, it was impossible!

Across the road, it was the hour at which a change of office guards took over from the old ones. Those who had come and those who were leaving were concluding their conversations as they kneaded lumps of chewing tobacco in their palms. As always, the building caretaker's massive greyhound had begun to prowl around the compound, licking the remnants of rice and meat scraps off its lips. Homi could clearly hear Priyadarshini, the newsreader, lovingly call out to the dog, 'Tiger, Tiger!'.

It was also time for a change of shift at the office, which meant young women and men were rushing in and out of the building. The cars that were picking up those on the night shift were drawing up inside the compound, and arrangements were being made to take those on the evening shift back to their homes. There was a chaos of vehicles inching forward or reversing, with an accompanying uproar. The women were doing most of the shouting in a bid to ensure they found places in cars that would take them home safely. And then, none of them wanted to be the last in any vehicle to be dropped off. Besides, each was in a hurry to get back, especially those who had husbands waiting.

It was different for the young men, such as Karan or Abhishek or Rahul or Aditya, all between 28 and 30 years old. After working all day under tremendous pressure, they didn't want to go back home right away. Their preferred destination was a pub or bar on Park Street or a restaurant in Chinatown. On Fridays and Saturdays they'd head for a nightclub, or a vacant flat belonging to a friend, where they could take their girlfriends and stay in bed like limp rags till ten in the morning. Every evening, those leaving the office had to contend with Mainuddin, who was in charge of all the cars, and who felt his sanity fray as he struggled to accommodate everyone's specific requirements.

On nights when she left after 10 PM, Homi took one of the cars on route six. She had been working continuously on the 12 noon-to-10 PM shift of late, without being allotted a morning shift. She had never been on night shift, as it hadn't been necessary.

She started her day so early that she usually had to slip on her jeans at 5 AM. But every morning over the past few months, even before fully waking up, she had felt the bed she shared with her husband turn into a ship and sail into deep but navigable waters, rolling gently from side to side; felt a pirate plundering her before she knew what was going on. She had often poked her fingers into the pirate's eyes, asking, 'How do you get so horny in your sleep?'

Hoisting her on top of himself, the pirate had replied, 'It's an automatic machine, not some cosmic consciousness or revolution.'

Those few minutes were so very good for life – so fulfilling. They were a pair of riders racing out of an unbarred stable, sitting on the same horse, holding the reins together. Their clothes slipped off by themselves as they galloped. On the edge of a ravine they stopped, now only whirling together, holding on to each other in fear, in excessive fear, the fear of plunging over the precipice. Or perhaps it was fear of the one she loved, whom she believed she loved completely. And yet at this moment, and every moment that succeeded it, Lalit seemed a stranger to her. When he ejaculated, Homi wondered whom he belonged to at the instant of orgasm – was it to her or to himself? Such nuanced questions, she knew, were never easy to answer.

It usually took Homi half an hour to get home on route six. The car dropped Pritha at Motilal Nehru Road, Tamas at Jatin Das Road, and then drove through back lanes to Hindustan Park, where Homi got off, after which it was the turn of Sumit, Vasudevan and Arjun. The names changed frequently, but that made no difference, for everyone kept their minds on their own homes. No one had any interest in striking up conversations with their fellow passengers. Someone like Pritha, whose child's nanny left at the stroke of eight, glanced at their watches constantly. Even if she was home by ten-thirty, it still meant her one-year-old daughter had to pass two-and-a-half hours under the supervision of her testy mother-in-law. On days when the child was more demanding than usual, crying and whining continuously, Pritha's husband pounced on her as soon as she returned.

Pritha entered the office every day determined to quit. But the moment Yash called her to the conference room to say, 'Pritha, the markets are crashing, twelve hundred points down, get hold of analysts and go live right now,' she forgot everything. Her family, husband, baby, mother-in-law, these existences were wiped out as she threw herself into work.

'Call Professor Mathur,' she urged her colleagues, 'we absolutely have to have him on the show.'

Standing in front of Jimmy's Kitchen, Homi remembered why she had crossed the road instead of getting into a Toyota Qualis or Tata Indica on route six. She had decided not to go home the usual way, but to return shortly before midnight, clasping Lalit's hand. Then they would hold each other and go to bed, impatiently lighting a candle meant to last all night, and sip some wine. As soon as the hands of the clock reached twelve Lalit would turn into a petitioner, touching her lips with his, and she would respond like a lapwing. A love affair would pass back and forth between their throats, the kind which was beyond expectations and quite wondrous, as rare as finding a specific grain of sand on the beach after a search which had made her suffer immensely, making her vulnerable. She had realised that a love affair was a myth created by the reality of the experiences she had gathered in the course of loving Lalit, and other people.

Lalit had said he would kiss Homi the way one blew a feather off one's palm. The kiss would drift into the air like powder, its particles falling in unison everywhere, on her shoulder, on her arms. Lalit would drain the honey from Homi's lips like a drunken butterfly. But first, he would meet her outside Jimmy's Kitchen and take her to Park Street. It would have to be an abbreviated dinner, for they simply had to get back home before twelve for the magical night they had planned. At the stroke of midnight Homi and Lalit would complete the first year of their being married. Six months of a thrilling romance had culminated in marriage exactly a year ago.

If, that is, there was such a thing as a 'culmination' in life.

It had taken her six months to leave Rudra and arrive at Lalit. As for the journey to Rudra from Arka via Rohit, with stopovers at Bitashok or some other person – how long had that taken? Six or seven years, possibly. A stretch of time during which a 'love affair' had seemed difficult to find.

Despite what had happened a short while ago, at a quarter-past-ten at night, here on AJC Bose Road, where she was now waiting for the greatest love of her life, the cranberry lipstick she had applied with great care before leaving the office was still smeared foolishly across her lips. Her heart continued to thump.

*Sink into my love…*

As soon as her mobile rang Homi knew Lalit was nearby. Shaking off her stupor, she answered, 'I'm waiting,' astonishing herself with the composure of her voice. She could not make up her mind whether it would be right to tell Lalit of the man with the matted locks tonight, at this moment. She even wondered whether it hadn't been an illusion. Maybe nothing had actually happened, and talking about it would make it real. She decided not to say anything. But she had no doubt that a disembodied being from a dream was clinging uncomfortably to her body.

The black car came into view as it turned left from Theatre Road. Homi got in when it drew up to her.

'You look different,' Lalit said even as Homi was climbing in. Did something happen? He was clearly in an excellent mood, without a trace of fatigue despite the backbreaking work he must have done all day. His collar was unwrinkled, his hair looked silken, and he was wearing a fine cologne. Despite his question, Lalit didn't appear particularly concerned. He must have assumed Homi had been told off at work, which was often the case thanks to her lethargy. Everyone knew how lazy she was. Just last week she had been assigned performance counselling with Anup Sinha from HR.

'If you have to accept me, Anup,' she'd told him pensively, 'you must accept me as I am. I'm lazy but not a shirker.'

Yash Vaidya, fiddling with his iPhone at the other end of the conference room, had chuckled at this.

Now that Lalit had asked, Homi could have told him everything. She had always considered desire the most important thing, and so never held back if there was something she wished to say. Still, she adopted a different strategy today.

'I was crossing the road, and an oil tanker almost ran me over.'

Lalit had switched on the indicator to signal that he would turn left into Park Street. But he slammed on the brakes instead, clamping his hand on Homi's arm.

'Seriously?'

She nodded silently.

'Really, Homi! A bus the other day, a tanker today. Why are you always so distracted?'

He touched her cheek.

'It scared you?'

She drew his hand to her left breast.

'Check for yourself.'

Her heart pounded harder at Lalit's touch. He kissed her forehead with a rueful sigh.

'How do I deal with this problem of yours, Khuku? Do I now have to worry about you being run over on an empty street? What were you thinking?'

'I don't want this kind of life, Lalit,' Homi exclaimed.

'What do you mean?'

Lalit sounded worried.

'I mean I don't want to die in a car accident.'

'Oh, well that's perfectly reasonable.'

'But what if that's what fate has in store for me?'

Homi did sound troubled. Lalit was genuinely surprised.

'Fate, accident, death, my god! You were *almost* run over, not actually.'

'Is that all that matters?' Homi pushed back.

They were at Park Street, from where they simply had to get home by midnight. Would they be able to order their dinner, eat it, and drive back home to Hindustan Park so as to be able to kiss exactly at 12? The uncertainty was exciting. It was as though they had thrown a challenge to the clock, like Homi usually did when travelling. She only ever made her flight or train by the skin of her teeth. The sensation that enveloped her during the ride to the station or the airport was one of overwhelming anxiety, which she positively savoured. On one occasion she had lost the gamble and missed her train, but that hadn't stopped her from playing over and over again.

As he parked the car, Lalit asked her once more how she was feeling.

Fat drops of rain began to fall as they entered the restaurant. It being July, rain was always on the cards. They sat facing each other on the first floor, their table nestling against a glass wall through which they could see Park Street flowing outside. No sooner had they taken their seats than the rain became torrential, blurring the view. Thick streams of water rolled down the glass, and the red and yellow lights of the cars outside merged with the anarchic currents of liquid, appearing as smudged dabs of colour on a translucent canvas. Homi gazed at the wall, forgetting even to blink. Suddenly a pair of covetous eyes materialised through the water and the light beams, eyes that she had seen barely half an hour ago. Homi was unable to speak.

Some time later she realised that Lalit had made a trip to the toilet and was now calling out to her.

'What's going on?'

Then he asked in irritation, 'Are you in one of your moods again, Khuku? It's a special day.'

'No, of course not,' Homi said. 'It's just …'

'It doesn't matter,' said Lalit. 'You're looking fantastic, by the way.'

He took a few photographs of her on his mobile phone. On the eve of her first marriage anniversary, Homi looked lonely, desolate, exhausted and distracted in each of them, even though she had had a quick wash back at the office and touched up her make-up before changing out of her shirt into a black silk top, added a golden belt, put on a different pair of shoes, and finished with a generous spritz of perfume.

She had done all of this with a singular focus, specifically for Lalit.

The make-up room had been almost empty at the time, all the assistants and hairdressers having left. It's only occupant was Priyadarshini, who had anchored the news from eight to ten that day, sitting there alone with her eyes closed.

'Going out with your husband?' she'd asked when she saw Homi.

Homi had nodded, smiling.

'Looking sexy,' Priyadarshini commented.

The look in the eyes of the smokers on the landing halfway down the stairs had told Homi the same thing.

'What a bomb,' Shamik had said.

'You could do yourself up like this for us, too, sometimes.'

Yet here she was less than an hour later – devastated.

A waiter lit Lalit's cigarette as soon as he held it between his lips.

'Want one?' Lalit asked.

'No,' she said.

'Order the food, ok? Get some prawns.'

Homi was struck with a sense of déjà vu. Everything had been the same the last time. A table next to the glass wall, the rain wiping everything away. When she picked up the menu she felt as though they were about to have the identical meal to before, that most events in her life were nothing but repetition. There was nothing truly original in existence besides birth and death. It was as though …

There are no eyes on the other side of the glass, Homi told herself. She had been mistaken. But her mind was in turmoil.

'You know, Lalit, I don't feel well enough to eat.'

Lalit's face stiffened instantly.

'You don't want to eat?'

'I feel funny.'

'Funny how?'

'I think someone's watching me. Stalking me.'

'Who?'

Lalit glanced around. Homi liked his protective air, it made her feel safe. 'I don't know who,' she said.

'But someone.'

'Is he inside the restaurant?' asked Lalit.

'No.'

Lalit leant back on the sofa.

'You'd better stop watching those horror movies every night.'

She grew despondent.

'You won't believe what happened today, Lalit.'

'I knew there was something. What, then?'

'A hermit ... while I was waiting for you ... he looked absolutely sex-starved. "Come to me," he said. He kept calling me. He was very attractive, you know. I wanted to go with him.'

Lalit's expression changed. In a low, restrained voice he said,

'What's the plan, Khuku? Do you want to ruin our night? You messed me up the same way on our wedding day. Which I'm okay with, you know, but it's not a joke anymore. We wanted to share our lives, didn't we, Khuku? But you simply cannot break out of your own little world, despite all the help I've given you. People like you, all you know is how to look after your own happiness.'

Lalit never missed the chance to say *people like you.*

Homi put her hands on her knees, a gesture of helplessness.

'I've given myself entirely to you, Lalit, believe me.'

'That's what you think.'

'I'm frightened, Lalit. I'm certain this hermit's here too.'

Suddenly Lalit's eyes grew tender, as they had many times in the past.

'People like you only want to take, Khuku, you

don't know how to give. You've no idea how tired I am today. I can barely sit upright. It's only for you that I ...'

Lalit stopped abruptly.

'Don't be afraid, Khuku, I'm here.'

'And what if one day you aren't?' she asked.

Lalit's gaze turned ice-cold.

'Is this really the best day to talk about such things, Khuku? Answer me.'

She had become stubborn now. As always.

Lalit held his hand out to her.

'Come, let's eat. We have to head home soon. It's raining cats and dogs.'

She looked out through the glass wall.

'Do you think we'll make it back before midnight?'

'Why not? We just need to leave by 11:30.'

'Maybe we won't make it, Lalit. Maybe the kiss you've saved for midnight will go to waste.'

'It won't', said Lalit. 'I'll kiss you at midnight wherever we happen to be. Come, sit next to me. Want me to feed you?'

'I don't do anything for you, Lalit,' she sobbed.

'But I love you madly.'

'I know,' Lalit told her.

It's time for some background details.

Homi and Lalit. One of them twenty-six years old, and the other, twenty-eight. A newly married couple. Homi had a postgraduate degree in English Literature from Jadavpur University. Lalit had an MBA from an institute in Bangalore. Homi had wound her way through different jobs into the media. Lalit had been in banking from the beginning. Both of them were seemingly ambitious, but they also liked to step outside the rat race now and then, or perhaps it was better to say that neither had entirely lost the youthful arrogance which allowed them to hit the pause button sometimes. Homi still toyed with the idea of academia, of stepping away from the glamorously eventful life of a media professional. Lalit could go abroad whenever he wanted. Even a move to Mumbai or Bangalore would mean doubling his earnings, but he preferred living in Kolkata. Both of them were highly emotional, often using their feelings to evaluate life. But these days Homi sensed that neither passion nor materialism held the upper hand in their lives. Each of these could, and did, substitute for the other at any given moment. But despite the similarities in their natures, the sacrifices to build and nurture their relationship were far greater on Lalit's part. In fact, it could be said that they fell to him almost entirely. Externally, Homi seemed an introvert. Cheerful, yes, but those who knew her well were aware of her penchant for negative thoughts. This made many people avoid her, from dislike or even fright.

When he said he knew that Homi loved him, a shadow of sadness had flitted across the face of the strapping, handsome, adventure-loving banker. Shaking it off, he frowned. 'I've not seen this top of yours before, Khuku. Talk about a plunging neckline!'

But Homi's attention was consumed by the hermit. Though the fear persisted, now, sufficient time had passed for a certain thrill to develop. Lalit speaking to her jolted her out of her thoughts, but it took a moment for her to process his question. She shook her head as she looked at him, as though trying to bring him into focus. Was their anniversary today or tomorrow? She couldn't remember. 'Rinki gave it to me,' Homi said eventually

Lalit didn't object to the neckline anymore after this. Rinki was his older sister. Though generally affable, Lalit's possessiveness asserted itself on certain occasions. Normally he didn't mind if Homi spent fourteen hours at work on weekdays. He paid no attention to what time she left and came back, or where she went in the meantime. But his mood turned foul whenever she had to go to work on

Sunday.

'Why did we bother to get married,' he would complain, 'if we can't even spend one day a week together?'

Sometimes Lalit put his foot down about her choice of clothes. He had no objection to Homi's revealing dresses when they were partying with his friends, but her own friends or an office party was another matter.

'Great show, Khuku,' he would say.

'You're giving them an eyeful these days, aren't you?'

Still, Homi could truthfully say that Lalit wasn't like most husbands. This side of him came out once a week at most.

There weren't many diners at the restaurant tonight, so they didn't have to wait long for their food. The sight of the succulent, steaming prawns even gave Homi the faint desire to eat. The clinking of cutlery blended with the muted background music. The light matched the sounds, a soft golden glow that didn't hurt the eye.

Looking at Lalit, Homi felt her skin prickling. Why had all this happened? If it was just a hallucination, why today of all days? This particular day would never come again, neither in her life nor in Lalit's.

She pleaded with herself to serve Lalit some of his favourite prawn dish. And it occurred to her that today's incidents were also the work of fate – nothing more. Everything was fated to have taken place just the way it had. This particular day hadn't shown itself suddenly but been been exposed, like ore laid bare after the rock containing it was eroded over time by storms and floods. Everything that was taking place was doing so thanks to fate, that irresistible puppeteer.

For the first time in her life Homi realised the meaning of the word, simultaneously aware of the presence of something intangible on her skin. Feeling that there was no oxygen in the air-conditioned restaurant, she began to cough.

'I don't want dessert, Lalit. We must get home by midnight.'

It was a challenge to the sensation on her skin.

It wasn't clear what Lalit made of this.

'We're leaving in ten minutes,' he said.

The rain had turned into a deluge by the time they left. Homi couldn't remember the last time she had seen such weather. The trees were ready to break. The raindrops seemed violent enough to make the windscreen shatter. They couldn't see a thing. And Lalit had turned the music up.

*I want you with no restraints, I am mad about you, my*

*love, with no restraints.*

He couldn't drive a minute without music.

She was screaming his name. He was laughing. How fast he was driving along the blurred roads – the man had no fear. Nor a fate of his own. Every time she asked him to slow down he let go of the steering wheel to kiss her hungrily. When he braked, the car seemed on the verge of overturning.

Meanwhile, they were running out of time. Homi was infected with excitement now. Her mercury was rising slowly. Ten to twelve. She was getting impatient.

'Will we make it?' she asked, her eyes on the road. Her voice was now that of a primordial lover.

'Of course.'

Lalit's jaw was set and his teeth were clenched.

It was three minutes to twelve when they escaped from the fury of the rain and drove into their complex of flats. Rather than wait for the lift, they raced up the stairs to the second floor. Homi's hands were shaking. Snatching the keys from her, Lalit unlocked the front door and shoved her inside, stepping swiftly in behind her. The wall clock struck twelve as he wrapped his powerful arms around her, sinking his lips onto hers. They had won. Homi, in particular.

The air whooshed out of her lungs as they kissed.

Their lips interlocked, their tongues danced together, they seemed to have found themselves just as they were about to be separated – that was how eloquent the kiss was, how well-supported by both of them. But the very next moment, Homi spotted him in the darkness of the balcony – the shadow of a half-naked man with matted locks. Standing there, unmoving. Their lips still pressed together, Homi grew rigid in Lalit's arms.

## A MARRIAGE ANNIVERSARY AND A FLASH OF FATALISM

Homi realised that whoever or whatever 'fate' might be, she was developing some sort of infatuation with it. Gazing at the blue arc inside the microwave oven, she tried to surmise its fate as well as her own.

The rain was still coming down in sheets – it hadn't let up since last night. The sky had a manic colour. And Papia, the part-time maid, had not turned up, leaving Homi unable to relax even though she had the day off. She and Lalit were supposed to be celebrating their anniversary with friends tonight.

It was raining, the fridge was empty, and Papia was absent – all the arrangements for ruining tonight's plans were in place. Homi did cook and clean on occasion, when the desire to do so struck her, but simply couldn't apply herself to such tasks when they were actually necessary. In such situations, the resentment she felt was too great.

They were married, but who was to say they ran a household? Homi and Lalit didn't go shopping regularly. And when they did, they ended up with precisely what they didn't need. Instead of detergent, Homi bought gardening tools. Or other things she liked: clothes, perfume, jewellery. Every time Lalit bought mushrooms, they had to be thrown away, because no one had remembered to cook them.

Neither she nor Lalit was capable of housework. She was too lazy, while Lalit preferred office work. They had married in order to be together – it had nothing to do with running a household. Of the two of them it was Lalit who was far more responsible, far less hot-headed, decidedly realistic. He didn't have a bad sense of humour, either. They had been renting this second floor flat in Hindustan Park for a year, and would be here two more years at the most. Lalit had already booked a twelve hundred square foot third floor flat in a new building coming up near Triangular Park. His father had given him a third of the price, which covered the advance payment. The rest of the money would come from a loan, which would be paid back during the long life that stretched ahead of him.

Lalit was the youngest of four, with two brothers and a sister. One of his brothers was several years older, and this brother's daughter was fourteen already. Having gone to boarding school since childhood, his connections with his parents, brothers and sister were tenuous at best. He had not claimed a share of the family house in New Alipur, asking his father for money instead, which nobody had objected to. Lalit's parents were so fond of his elder brother Pramit's wife Mitul that they didn't want another daughter-in-law in the family. Besides, Lalit's mother had decided at the outset to ignore Homi – she had not considered Homi's background satisfactory.

In the early days of their marriage, Homi would stir herself to pick a suitably demure outfit whenever Lalit said he was going to New Alipur. But after a few visits Lalit had told her to not to bother.

'No need for you to go every time,' he'd said. 'Only when absolutely essential.'

Homi had jumped up to kiss him. She no longer remembered the last family visit. Given Homi and Lalit's lifestyle, a household was nothing more than a side order. The main course, inevitably and indispensably, was love.

These days everyone talked about not wasting or misusing the earth's resources. Save water, save energy – these were the constant slogans from environmentalists. Homi took herself to task for getting distracted and forgetting to switch the microwave off in time. She had been working on this very subject for the past two weeks. Her lifestyle programme would show how Kolkata's top businessmen, industrialists and corporate bosses were trying to curtail their use of electricity and water, efforts which had themselves become a sort of status symbol.

Papia had left a tray with all the arrangements for making tea. Putting the kettle on, that was something Homi could do. She could once again hear the rainfall which she had become oblivious to because of her web of thoughts. Torrential rain.

By the light of day, Homi had classified the previous night's frightening incident as largely imagined, though her heart shrank every time she recalled that pair of eyes. Leaning back against the kitchen wall, she sighed – could she really tell herself that it was all in her mind? What was the source of all this fear? And what would its outcome be?

Homi went into the bedroom with a cup of tea to wake Lalit. He hadn't yet stirred after the sex last night, and was still sleeping on his stomach, naked. Lalit had been so aroused last night that he hadn't even noticed Homi stiffening at the presence of a third entity. It wasn't only fear she'd felt, but the queasy sensation of someone watching them make love. She had felt so very helpless, but hadn't dared say anything to Lalit. How much could a man in the prime of his life tolerate? How much generosity was he supposed to demonstrate? And how would he get rid of an imaginary stalker, in any case? So Homi had said nothing. Lalit had toyed with her body, slamming her down on the bed, dragging her into a sitting position, even forcing her to stand. She had responded like a marionette, but there was no sexual energy within her, no desire to return his kisses, no power to clasp Lalit's hand and ride the wave as it washed up on the shore. His frenzied foreplay only made her feel lonely.

Thinking back on it now, Homi felt contrite. She pressed her cheek to Lalit's back, her head moving now to the rhythm of his breathing. After a while, Lalit woke up. Groping like a blind man, he touched her, saying, 'Come to me.'

Homi was electrified. She sprang to her feet like a soldier under orders. Her head reeled. She moved to a corner of the room, one hand on the wall for support, suddenly feeling so panic-stricken that she wanted to leave the flat at once. To get a grip on herself, she went to the basin by the dining table and splashed some water on her face.

'The rain doesn't look like stopping today, Khuku,' Lalit called from the bedroom, still sounding half–

asleep.

'What can I do about it?' Homi muttered.

'It's hard to tell where this is going.'

Lalit was probably sitting up in bed now, pouring himself a cup of tea.

'Khuku?'

Homi didn't feel like going near him. She stood there gnawing at her fingernails.

After calling out to her a couple of times, Lalit emerged from the bedroom, naked, his cup of tea in one hand, a cigarette between his lips. Homi didn't need to look to know his penis was drooping now. The virile sex that her husband/lover bestowed on her, the flaming pleasure she experienced like a spark alighting on gunpowder – she felt convinced that this man would never again provide any such sensations. Lalit gripped her arm.

'Khuku? Is everything ok, baby?'

In a sudden burst of heartlessness, Homi said,

'If I ever want to leave you, Lalit, please don't ask me why. I won't, if it's the other way around ...'

A mixture of amusement and anger settled slowly on Lalit's arched eyebrows. He shrugged elaborately, laughing.

'God is great, yaar. I thought we were about to celebrate our anniversary, but here we are, talking of separation instead. Great!'

Lalit kept shaking his head.

'I know you're unpredictable, Khuku, I know you talk before you think, you do as you please up – but I'm slowly discovering you're cruel too.'

He slammed the bathroom door behind him.

It took Homi only a second or two to realise she had committed a blunder. What she had done was unacceptable. She had said something she had never wanted to say.

Was doing something against one's will, saying what one didn't want to, also a matter of fate?

Homi banged on the bathroom door.

'I didn't mean to hurt you, Lalit. If only you knew all that I've been going through since last night.'

'You're right, I don't know, and I don't understand, either,' Lalit said from the other side of the door. Homi broke down.

'You never get this angry.'

'Calm down,' Lalit said after a pause.

'No need to get so upset. Let me come out and talk to you.'

Homi wandered out to the balcony, where she had arranged some plants from the Horticultural Garden. All had died from lack of care. The place looked horrible. This was the spot where she had seen the hermit standing last night, still as a statue. Homi decided to throw the pots away as soon as Papia turned up. Her stalker, and the scraggy limbs of the dead plants were pieces of the same puzzle – or so it seemed to her.

Hearing sounds in the bedroom, Homi went back inside to face Lalit. But he looked as though nothing had happened.

'Have you thought about how you'll manage tonight?' he asked. 'You'll have to go shopping, won't you? What are you going to feed the guests?'

Homi put her hand on Lalit's chest.

'You tell me. I'll do exactly as you ask me to from now on. I won't torture you like this anymore. I won't say foolish things.'

Lalit raised his eyebrows. 'You'll keep your thoughts to yourself?'

Homi hesitated. Taking her hands in his, Lalit brought them together.

'Some women are like flowers, they can get away with murder. Go on, make my life as difficult as you want to. I'm ready for it.'

'You won't leave me, even if I go mad?'

'Why should you go mad?'

'I did, once, in my childhood. That's a fact.'

Lalit moistened his lips with his tongue. His eyes grew cold and dry. Homi felt he was the only guardian she had. About the same age as she was, yet so much older.

'All our childhoods are actually forms of madness,' Lalit said. 'There's just one thing you have to remember. We've built a relationship, a beautiful relationship, which has an existence in reality, where there is room for reason and evidence. As long as you can hold on to that reality, that reason, everything will be fine, you'll see.'

Homi's eyes were brimming over with tears.

'I'm your daughter, all right, Lalit?'

'You're my daughter,' Lalit agreed.

'We won't have another daughter.'

'No.'

'Happy anniversary.' Finally, Homi found herself able to say it.

Her mood improved immediately. Dressed in a pair of shorts and a baggy T-shirt, Homi poured vermilion powder onto her parting, slid glass bangles onto both arms all the way up to her elbows, fixed a dot on her forehead, hooked danglers on her ears, put on some lipstick, and began to dance.

'Listen,' she said, 'that bitch Papia hasn't turned up. The fridge is empty, and it's raining. I don't even remember how many people you've invited.'

Lalit had picked up his camera and was snapping

shots of Homi. He was obsessed with taking pictures. If he liked something, he wasn't happy unless he could see it again later in the form of a photograph.

'All right then, let's go shopping,' he said. 'Adesh and Tultul are coming too, it's a huge crowd. How much booze do you think we need to pick up?'

'I'll go as I am now, Lalit,' Homi said.

'Sure, just put on a pair of jeans.'

Homi's phone rang. *Sink into my love.*

'Yes Ma, tell me,' Homi spoke into the phone. Her mother made it a point to call her every day.

'What are you doing?'

This question was a routine one and in bad taste.

Homi stopped dancing. Lalit put his camera away, lit a cigarette and stepped out of the room.

Killing her ebullience and sitting down on the bed, Homi said, 'Just had some tea.'

'Kolkata's under water, Khuku. They're showing the streets on your channel. I'm sure your maid, that migratory bird, hasn't turned up.'

'No, Ma, she hasn't.'

'Mine's disappeared for three days now. Including today. No news, no information. The audacity of her! How dare she do this to me, Khuku?'

Homi was silent.

'I'm going to plant a kick on her ass when she

does turn up. Listen, I need someone immediately.'

Her mother was ordering her.

'Don't sack her till you find a replacement,' Homi warned. 'You know how tough it is to get a maid these days.'

'I can't tell you what a bitch she is. The way she beats my muslin clothes tears the fabric. I've told her over and over again to take more care. The other day I asked her to pluck some neem leaves for me, you know what she did? She practically pulled the plant out of the pot and gave me the brownest leaves she could find. And then her constant demands. Give me a sari, give me Didi's old clothes. Give me a raise. The greed of her! You know how much I pay her? Two thousand, no less.'

It wasn't as though any of this maid's predecessors had been lacking in the departments of greed and dishonesty.

'Look, Ma ...,' Homi tried, and her mother seemed to get the point.

'Never mind, so what's your plan tonight? How many guests?'

'I'm not sure yet. About eleven or twelve.'

'Now that you've gone and married someone your own age, you'll have to wait at least five years to get membership of a club. And even then there's no guarantee either. How can anyone manage without a club membership? You'll run up a bill of thirty thousand if you have fifteen people drinking. Listen, Khuku, just order in tonight and heat it up in the microwave. Maybe make a salad yourself.'

'Let's see, I might have to do just that. There's plenty of time.'

'That's what I've been doing these past three days. Just ordering in and heating it up. I can't get involved in cooking anymore, Khuku. I don't care if it upsets your father not to have home-cooked food.'

Homi smiled.

'When has Baba ever been upset with you?'

'What do you know? You should have seen his veins swelling when I asked him to wipe the table yesterday.'

Homi couldn't visualise her father with swollen veins. Although just then, she couldn't even recall his face. Changing her tone, her mother said,

'Did you know Mr Banerjee lost his power of speech the night before last? Oli and Tejen are coming by this evening's flight.'

Homi listened in silence.

'It doesn't seem like he'll survive,' her mother continued.

Mr Banerjee was Homi's mother's first husband,

whom she had married at twenty and divorced at thirty. The separation was itself now thirty years old. Her mother had married her father and given birth to Homi despite dithering over whether to have a child or not. Oli and Tejen were her daughter and son-in-law from the first marriage. Even if Mr Banerjee were to die now, after being confined to his bed for two years, it wouldn't bring any change to her mother's life, Homi thought. Till the very last day, the man would be as irrelevant as he had been for the past thirty years. Likewise, her mother's bonds of loathing with Mr Banerjee and his family would remain unchanged. And amidst all this there would be Oli, the daughter Homi's mother preferred to her.

These bonds cannot be understood easily. They have to be described in detail.

Oli on the phone from Bombay: 'Ma, do you know the things Rangapishi is saying about me?'

'Your father's sister? What is she saying?'

Their mother was livid even before hearing the details.

'That I was rummaging in Baba's locker for his papers during my last visit. That I took some jewellery. You know the truth, Ma, do I even care for their jewellery? Have they gone mad? Who do they think they're accusing? Don't they know who I am? Has

Rangapishi even *seen* the kind of jewellery I own?'

Of course, all this was just swagger. Oli had married someone from a very rich and renowned Bombay family while studying in London. She was forty now, and 'affluence' didn't begin to describe the wealth she had married into. Her house was practically a palace. But still she would poke around in her mother's cupboard and jewellery-box every time she came home. Last time she had pleaded tearfully to be allowed to take a dozen of her mother's pure gold bangles. Although, being the only child, she had no competitor for her inheritance, she was too impatient to wait for her father to die. Their mother was constantly urging Oli to persuade him to bequeath his property to her. But Mr Banerjee – a man who wore wooden clogs in the house, used a traditional brass pot to bathe, ate nothing but steamed rice, and never entered into conversation with anyone except the servants – had not relinquished his assets despite spending the past two years confined to his bed. All of Oli's efforts had failed. Their mother feared that his sisters were responsible, that they had advised him to refuse Oli's entreaties. Each sister was a witch as far as Oli's mother was concerned; they had made her suffer immensely when she had been Mr Banjeree's wife. Now they were intent on depriving Oli of her inheritance so they could seize it for themselves.

Weeping, Oli would release a stream of complaints, at which her mother would pound her fist on the table.

'Stop this whining, Oli. You've done nothing wrong, even if you did take the jewellery – the point is, have you been able to tell them as much? If you haven't, I never want to see you again, you can crawl before your beloved aunts and beg for forgiveness, you can return everything you've taken.'

'I didn't take anything, Ma,' Oli would say

'Then go tell them that,' her mother would respond even more angrily.

'Ma, Rangapishi said Baba told them I did it. I called Baba at once, and he wouldn't listen to anything I had to say. You know what he told me? Don't enter this house before my death, Oli. Can you imagine treating your only child this way? I neglected my own family to take care of him for an entire month. Is this how he pays me back? How could Baba say this to me?'

'Who cares if he said it? That's nothing to cry over. What you should have said is, which of your loving sisters will inform me when you do pass away? They'll be busy grabbing their share of the spoils. How those women tormented me! And your father! A slave to his sisters. Do you think I wasn't pretty, Oli? But to your father there's no one in the world more beautiful than his sisters. My god! The truth is that your Rangapishi wants Mr Banerjee to leave the Sunny Park flat to her younger son. You're such a fool, you don't even see it.'

The kind of humiliation that Oli's mother heaped on her from time to time also deserves description.

'Can you imagine, Khuku, Tejen's in Kolkata but I haven't been told! What's the idea of insulting me like this?'

'Really? Tejen's in Kolkata?'

Oli and Homi had never paid much attention to each other. Their mother had never encouraged any kind of real relationship between them – as though the fact that the same woman had given birth to them both was entirely irrelevant. And besides, Oli had left to study in London when Homi was just five, then got married and went off to live with her husband. Homi still remembered Oli's wedding, which had counted many famous names, even ministers, among the guests. Her mother had bought her father tickets to the seaside at Puri. And Homi had spent the entire week playing with the nanny's daughter.

Whenever Oli and her children came to stay at their Belvedere Road house, Homi would shut herself in her second-floor room, only emerging when absolutely necessary.

The conflict had always raged within their mother – did Oli belong to her, or to the Banerjee family? When Oli visited, no one noticed if Homi disappeared altogether. But then Oli was Oli, born into a family of wealthy landowners, stunningly beautiful, educated in London, a daughter-in-law of the Patils. How could Homi be compared to her? They had a mother in common, and that was all – a mother whose CV matched her elder daughter's, for her own father had been a barrister. A student of Loreto Convent, Darjeeling, she was the sole heir of her father's property. The Belvedere Road house had belonged to her parents. After marrying Homi's father, a professor whom she'd met when he was Oli's private tutor, she had prevailed on him to move into this house. Homi herself had been born within its walls, but she and her father had always lived there on sufferance, dependent on her mother's support. Excluded from her social circles, they had lived a kind of refugee life.

Oli and her mother actually belonged to the kind of family whose members, even today, would, when angry, scream things like, 'I'll have you thrown out,' or, 'I'll have you shot'.

Apparently Mr Banerjee used to play the esraj after such temper tantrums. Homi's mother loved nothing more than to talk of the illustrious family from which she had been separated for thirty years. When it came to Homi and her father, she had rather less to say.

The long and the short of it was that Homi addressed Tejen as Tejen, and Oli as Oli. She did not acknowledge any relationship with them.

'And how did you know Tejen's in Kolkata?' Homi asked.

'From Sukhen, of course.'

Sukhen was Mr Banerjee's man Friday, but he was also Homi's mother's spy. His primary task was to inform her of everything that happened at Sunny Park.

'If only you knew why Tejen's here!'

She was bubbling with excitement now.

'Well, why is he?' Homi had no choice but to ask.

'To appease Mr Banerjee, what else. Oli sent him. *"Baba's angry with me. He won't let me into the house. You have to go and explain."* So the ass has actually flown in to persuade his father-in-law. Oli wants to have her cake and eat it, too. I know my daughter only too well. She can't sleep at night for fear of losing out on her father's property. She's every bit as selfish and evil as the rest of her family, Khuku. The last time she was visiting Dyuti in Milan, I begged her to bring me a pair of walking shoes. I've been using the ones she got me for over a year now. When I was out the other day Ranjana Poddar said, "You need to change your shoes, Mrs Banerjee, the soles are worn out." I was mortified. Should I tell her that my daughter said, *"Sorry Ma, there was no room, I'll bring a pair next time"*? She goes abroad on shopping sprees at the drop of a hat, but everything she buys is for herself. Bloody bitch!'

Dyuti was Oli's daughter, in Italy to study fashion design. Homi's father's was called Nabobrata Dutta, but her mother had been Mrs Banerjee ever since the age of twenty.

'The truth is she's a miser, Khuku, won't spend a rupee more than she has to.'

As though their mother was any different. She refused to hire a cook or a full-time driver for the family car. The few times she'd been prevailed upon, she'd never managed to get along with them more than twenty-four hours. Then the usual – quarrels, accusations, swearing. Homi had grown up with her mother's outbursts, while her father had grown old with them. Ever since Homi could remember, her father would sit in his room with the doors closed, never coming out, never speaking, never even eating. He was little more than skin and bones, his vision was blurred, and his arms and legs shook. There was a rattle in his throat.

'Your father is insane,' Homi's mother told her once. 'I didn't realise it at first. By the time I did, it was too late – he'd already married me and planted himself in this house.'

Homi tried to maintain some distance from her mother. Her father, she simply despised. Not anger, not pity, but hatred. Because she knew very well that he was not insane at all, merely selfish, lazy, a shirker. There was nothing sad about his situation – it was his preferred mode of living. Marrying her mother had enabled him to adopt this existence.

Even a half-hour conversation with her mother exhausted Homi. She couldn't take it anymore these days. The way Lalit took care of her had changed her greatly. She wanted to cling to him like a shadow, to be serene and graceful. Lalit knew that communication with her family devastated Homi, and he disliked her foul-mouthed mother deeply. He had never come out and said it, but Homi knew that he wanted her to cut all ties with Belvedere Road.

'When are you taking me to the dentist, Khuku? How much longer do I have to suffer?'

Finally, Homi's mother had come to the point.

'He's given us an appointment for the day after tomorrow. Seven-thirty in the evening. You'd better inform the driver.'

'Don't talk to me about drivers. There was one who came the other day ...'

Homi itched to throw the phone across the room.

'... but then Oli's arriving today, let's see what happens. Mr Banerjee won't last much longer. I'm terrified, Khuku – Oli will be a wreck when she gets here. She puts on such a fine act, but she's already bagged everything she wanted to, there's no purpose to be served with tears anymore. It's true, there's nothing left in the locker. Oli ransacked it the last time Mr Banerjee was ill. I had all the details from Sukhen. He'd been guarding madam's jewellery with his life – now Oli has it all.'

Homi's mother referred to her former mother-in-law as madam.

She had been bitterly opposed to the idea of Homi's marrying Lalit. Atul Kashyap of Satyam & Co., who had fallen in love with Homi around the same time, had sent a marriage proposal through Oli. Homi had even gone on a date with Atul after a quarrel with Lalit, but then quickly made up with and married Lalit, possibly within the next seven days. Her mother had never been more deflated. But who knew how she would have reacted if it had happened ten years earlier? Likely it would have been far more explosive.

Age was certainly a factor. These days, Mrs Banerjee was frequently short of breath.

Homi's life with Lalit had its own rhythm. It took her a little time to return to it after her mother hung up. After some discussion, they decided to order in the food for the guests that night. Lalit would go out in the afternoon to get the drinks and some snacks, then make another trip later to pick up the dinner. While these plans were being made, Homi made salami sandwiches with mustard. They would have had a more elaborate breakfast had Papia shown up. When the subject of lunch came up she stretched so exaggeratedly that Lalit snapped his fingers, saying, 'Khichuri! I'll cook.'

There wasn't much to be done now. The guests were basically Lalit's friends from college and work, for Homi had no real friends of her own. She was on good terms with everyone, but couldn't progress beyond a certain level of intimacy. She knew that people became demanding when friendship turned into a relationship, and she didn't care for commitments. But then how did she manage her job? She did manage it, and she could, by projecting an image of herself as a creative type, so that no one interfered with her work.

Homi did some dusting, replaced the everyday

bedcover with a fancier one, rearranged the cushions on the drawing room sofa, filled the ice trays, made sure the toilet freshener was topped up, put in fresh towels, and took what little crockery they possessed out of the cabinet to set the dining table. Then she went to the bathroom to wash her hair.

She had just turned on the shower when Lalit began hammering on the door.

'Open up.'

'What is it?'

She opened the door.

'What are you up to?' Lalit asked, his Adam's apple bobbing, a broad grin on his face. 'He's such a child,' Homi thought to herself. Just likes to pretend he's grown up.

'What do you suppose?' she said, darting back to the hot shower without closing the door – she was prone to catching colds.

Lalit quickly stripped off his clothes and entered the bathroom, naked.

'Let me shampoo your hair, Khuku,' he begged. 'And your khichuri?'

Her eyebrows danced.

'Please, please, please.' Lalit was close enough now that the shower spray wet him.

'Damn it, you'll get shampoo in my eyes.'

'I won't, I swear.'

Seeing Lalit's reddened lips, Homi realised that the shampoo was just an excuse. Clearly the blood flow in his body had peaked. And all his hopes, desires, lust, and love had taken shelter in one small area. It was getting harder by the minute, touching Homi's belly, thighs, knees, buttocks. Two lean, youthful, active physical beings – always ready for sex.

Finally the beige marble floor offered refuge to both of them. And that was when it happened. Homi was groping for Lalit's head to pull it to her breast when she shocked herself with the realization that she had subconsciously been seeking something else – a much larger head, one with matted locks and a necklace of beads around its neck. A gigantic, heavy head, sitting on a colossal body, in comparison to which Lalit's own head was light as a feather. A silken, unnavigable nothing, it could even be called a void. Homi's desire suddenly appeared directionless. She felt she had always been seeking a head charged with sexuality, but had never found one. Not Rudra, not Bitashok, not Lalit – none of them had proven capable. Her imagination had remained just that, imagination. It had neither been overthrown nor made material. She saw her feelings about Lalit changing every moment. Homi closed her eyes in fear.

After sex in the shower, followed by lunch, Homi was lying in bed next to Lalit, who was running his fingers through her hair. She fell asleep, only to be woken by the ringing of her phone. She had to drag herself forcibly out of her stupor. Her heart was heavy, she realised. It was five in the evening, and the rain had stopped. Lalit was asleep, a book lying face down on his chest. It was her mother calling, of course. Would she have to hear another rant about Oli? Or had Mr Banerjee finally died?

'What, Ma?' Homi snapped, unable to suppress her irritation.

'Khuku … Khuku … something's wrong with him.'

Homi couldn't understand who her mother was talking about

'It's your father, Khuku. Something's wrong. He's fallen off the bed, his eyes are fixed, he's foaming at the mouth.'

'Lalit, Lalit,' Homi screamed.

# FATE'S TRYST

It took Homi and Lalit less than ten minutes to get dressed and leave. Homi called their family doctor from the car. Her mother had spoken to him already.

'The ambulance has just left with Mr Dutta,' Dr Ghosh informed her. 'You can go directly to the hospital. I've asked Mrs Banerjee to stay at home, Homi. I don't think she's needed there.'

'Is Baba still alive, uncle?' asked Homi.

'Yes, he is.'

'Call Ayesha,' Lalit said.

Homi did, at once.

'Ayesha, my father is seriously ill. We're on our way to the hospital. We have to cancel the party.'

'Of course!' Ayesha exclaimed.

'Do me a favour, please call the other guests for me and let them know.'

'Don't worry, I'll take care of it. Is there anything else I can do?'

'Not right now, but I'll tell you if I think of anything.'

It took over half an hour to complete the formalities at the hospital. Rushing between different departments, they learnt that the doctors suspected a cerebrovascular attack, and so the patient had been sent for an MRI. They couldn't tell Homi anything concrete until 72 hours had passed. After the MRI, as Mr Dutta was being taken to the Intensive Care Unit, Homi got a good look at her father's face for the first time in nearly a year.

They ran into Dr Ghosh in the corridor outside the ICU.

'Listen, Homi,' he said, 'this is serious. We're doing everything we can, let's see what happens. Let me know the moment they tell you anything, and I'll talk to the consultant straight away. All right?'

Dr Ghosh walked off with Lalit. The waiting area was so crowded that there wasn't a chair to be had. Homi stood leaning against the wall, a tense figure with dry eyes. In this lifetime at least, she wouldn't be able to shut out the image of an inert body whenever she thought of her father. A man with his pride taken away, a father but not a guardian, handsome but a coward, averse to working, someone who had never offered Homi an ounce of affection, preferring to hide his face behind a book instead. Homi remembered one particular day when she had seen that the door to his room was open, and had been about to enter. Her father had been getting out of his pyjama bottoms, and his scrawny legs were visible. He had slammed the door in her face, and she heard the detestable sound of him clearing his phlegm-clogged throat.

That she had rushed to the hospital held absolutely no significance. There were no personal feelings involved – when it came to her father, she was the victim of a mental void. She knew that it didn't matter to anyone whether her father lived or died, not even to him.

It occurred to her as she stood there that different destinies were intertwined in this whole business. Take her father's illness – it involved her own fate, her father's, and her mother's. In fact, if you thought about it, the fate of the entire world was linked to this man, her father. The nurse over there, adjusting the drip attached to his arm – Mr Dutta's illness was her fate too, since it affected the course of her life in some way. But everything in this woman's life was controlled by her own fate. Did everyone share a collective fate, then? Was every event in the world actually part of a single event? But the hermit with the horrifying appearance had claimed he was her, Homi's, fate. Could he be her fate alone, and no one else's?

As these thoughts ran through her head, Homi wondered whether death would make a choice between Mr Banerjee and Mr Dutta. Mr Banerjee's final hour had been creeping closer for a long time, and was now at the door, whereas Mr Dutta had at least 72 hours in hand, according to the doctors. And yet, he hadn't even been ill till a few hours ago, and was younger than Mr Banerjee. But now there was some bleeding in his brain.

Her mother's current or former husband – which of the two would death accept first? How would their respective destinies compete or cooperate with each other? Or would both of them make it through unscathed this time, thanks to the vagaries of fate?

As Homi sat down on a sofa that had become vacant, she realised that the word 'fate' was gathering in her heart like unshed tears, gnawing away at her. A tall hermit with a noble brow had enveloped her in some sort of sorcery, demanding intimacy with her. And the air around her had become heavier, making the indirect sensation palpable.

—

It was Lalit who did all the work. Homi sat quietly, drank a cup of coffee, went out for a cigarette, and returned to find her seat taken. She had no words of hope to offer her mother every time the latter called.

'I think I'll go to bed, Khuku,' Mrs Banerjee said at last. 'I've been feeling sick ever since I saw your father in that state. The jackfruits have ripened so much that their smell is overpowering. I wish I could send for someone to pluck them, but who? There isn't even anyone here to make a cup of tea. I told the tenants' servant, get me some tea, will you – so you see how bad things are here. He was dripping with politeness, said he'd send me a cup at once, but there's no sign of it. I'm starving too, all I had in the afternoon was ...'

All her talk was leaving her short of breath.

'Has Oli landed, Ma?' Homi asked.

'She went straight to Sunny Park from the airport. What are you doing there, Khuku? Come over. Lalit can manage.'

Even if Homi left the hospital she had no intention of going to her mother's house, to the smell of jackfruits. She would go wherever divine providence took her. She had begun to accept the idea of fate, the same fate which had despatched Lalit and her to the hospital on their wedding anniversary. Yes, all of this must have been predestined.

But although Homi was determined not to visit her mother, eventually, she had to give in. She and Lalit had left the hospital around ten at night for dinner, meaning to return to the waiting area, where they planned to spend the night nodding off in the company of hundreds of anxious relatives and friends.

'Go to your mother's,' Lalit had said, 'I'll stay here.'

She hadn't agreed.

After they had eaten their sandwiches and drunk their coffee at a nearby restaurant, Lalit had some sandwiches packed for her mother before Homi had the chance to intervene. Then they went to Belvedere Road, which was just two minutes away. The servant downstairs opened the gate for them. Homi had a set of keys to the collapsible gate guarding the first floor, but her mother came out as soon as she heard them, dressed in dirty pyjama bottoms and a T-shirt. She disappeared instantly, returning with a housecoat wrapped around herself. Homi made a flask of coffee while Lalit talked with Mrs Banerjee, and poured her mother a cup.

'Will he get better, Khuku?' she asked. 'Or will he be a cripple, pissing and shitting in his bed? Who's going to look after him, Khuku?'

'It's too early to think of all that, aunty,' said Lalit. 'We'll get trained nurses and caregivers if need be.

Don't worry – you won't have to do it yourself.'

Homi's mother had been dazzlingly beautiful in her youth. The loveliness had evaporated, but the dazzle had remained. Her pout had disappeared, but the arch looks were still there. She gave Lalit one of them now.

'The thing is, Lalit, I need my afternoon nap. How can I have a cripple disturbing me?'

Lalit had used to look at her in consternation when she said such things. Now, he couldn't tolerate her for long.

'You live so far away,' she complained as Homi and Lalit were leaving. 'Do civilized people even live in rented flats?'

They were only saved from further pronounce-ments because Oli called again.

In the car, turning the ignition on, Lalit shook his head. 'What a woman! Amazing! Incredible!'

Homi rolled with laughter in her seat.

—

She and Lalit spent almost the entire night next to each other in the lounge outside the ICU. Lalit dozed off, as did many of the other patients' relatives. There were always a few pacing up and down, or making a trip to the toilet. Then at one point Homi saw her hermit, distinct beneath the bright white ceiling lights – her fourth vision. The look in his eyes, his expression, his jaw, his build – all added up to an inexplicable presence. Homi shrank back in fear, feeling the urge to scream, to have people gather around, to throw herself at Lalit. But not a sound escaped her lips. She couldn't lift her arm, couldn't even twitch a finger. Her feet were rooted to the ground. The man stared at her with ghoulish desire in his eyes.

'Get out of here, Homi, run away!' she told herself. But there was no response in her besides the hair on her body standing on end. The man with the matted locks held his hand out towards her, his arm impossibly long. Yesterday, when she hadn't yet known he was her fate, she had been able to be angry. Today, things were different – she knew his dreadful role in her life.

'Why? Why? Why are you pursuing me?' she wanted to ask him.

'I haven't questioned any of the things in my life in any way that might make you want to remind me of your existence, to show your strength, to demonstrate how, next to you, I am nothing. Whether Lalit and I celebrate our wedding anniversary makes no difference to me, the death of neither Mr Dutta nor Mr Banerjee will have any impact, even losing Lalit wouldn't make me complain. I have no great ambition, no desire to travel around the world, no anxiety about being killed in a bomb explosion. I don't have anything to protest against, I let things happen as they will.'

At this point, she realised a contradiction in her thoughts.

'It's true, though, that you can stalk me if you like. Why should I object? The thing is, I'm afraid of you. Very well, I'll be afraid of you. Yes, I'll be afraid.'

She saw the man's eyes turn even more grotesque, saw his lips moving hungrily behind his beard and moustache. She summoned all her strength to screw her eyes shut – which was when someone shook her shoulder to get her attention. A grave, middle-aged nurse.

'Your father's recovered consciousness. But we're putting him back to sleep. You can see him through the glass wall over there.'

Homi stood up and began to follow the nurse, when her phone rang.

'Mr Banerjee is gone, Khuku, just a few moments ago.'

Homi stopped in her tracks.

'Oh,' she murmured. Looking around, she could no longer see the hermit.

Her mother didn't ask after Mr Dutta. All she said was, 'Oli's insisting I should be with her.'

A daughter asking her mother to be with her after her father's death. Surely such a request was only natural. Homi spoke to her mother candidly for once.

'You must go, Ma.'

'But how can I go to Sunny Park after all these years, Khuku? The entire clan will be gathered there – all those bitches and their drama. They're going to wish I was dead.'

'You're not going in order to see them.'

'Of course I'm not. My daughter needs me. She wants to hold my hand, she needs my shoulder to cry on. After all, a death is death, Khuku.'

Homi glanced over at the glass wall the nurse had indicated. As far as she knew, her father had no other family of his own. And yet he would probably survive. She had been prepared to witness fate in action. Yet it was Mr Banerjee who had died, while Mr Dutta had regained consciousness – though the judgment on whether he would survive or die had not yet been pronounced.

# A VERY STRANGE LOVE AFFAIR

Ten days later, as she was walking past the National Library on her way back from the hospital, Homi sensed someone following her. Close behind. As she sped up or slowed down, so did her stalker. Homi didn't even bother to turn around – it was obvious who it was.

It was seven-thirty in the evening. Lalit had been on a business trip for the past two days, and would be away for about ten more. Every morning on her way to work and every evening on her way back, Homi went to the hospital by herself to see her father. She discussed his condition with the doctors, bought the medicines prescribed, waited despondently in the lounge, and watched an avalanche of visitors descend as soon as the sun declined, all by herself.

There had been no improvement in her father's condition in ten days. He wasn't moving, his eyes were half-closed and unfocused, and no words ever rose to his lips – no sounds at all, in fact. But he wasn't unconscious. He was asleep, a deep, seemingly pain-free slumber. A peaceful sleep which, Homi thought, he had been seeking for a long time. No one but Lalit asked after him now. Her mother had only said,

'Do what you think best, Khuku.'

There was a lot of traffic in front of the National Library. Huge buses and sleek minibuses were roaring past, the lights never changing to red. Homi marched up and down the pavement, trying to spot an open-ing in the traffic so she could cross the road. There were no other pedestrians nearby. Standing on a street which seemed suspended in a smoky yellow light, she experienced a strange sense of personal freedom. At the same time, the sensation seemed to indicate that she had never in any of her lives been alone, that there had always been someone with her, someone who was with her now and always would be. She would have to spend her life with this infinitely unreal entity. She wondered whether her stalker would confront her today as well, whether he would again address her as Empress.

He no longer disconcerted her. Instead of taking a taxi, she began to walk along the darkened road towards Alipur Jail. Yes, there were footsteps behind her. Bushes and shrubs lined the pavement here, and he was walking close to them. She stopped, resumed walking, stopped, resumed walking. Eventually she turned left into the narrow road which curved around the wall of the jail. At every moment she expected the hand with the rosary beads around the wrist to fall on her shoulder. And when it did, Homi would ask, 'What now?'

She lost track of how far she had walked. At one point, she realised she had reached the crowded street in front of Jagu Bazaar. Jostled by people shouting at the tops of their voices, she suddenly felt bewildered, and exhausted. It was a quarter past eight. She would have to cross the road again to return to her office. The weather was oppressively sultry, with clouds looming overhead – it was bound to rain. No, she wouldn't go back to work. Or should she? What would she do at home, anyway? She looked around like a child, as though in search of instructions on an advertising board. For she could no longer think for herself. There he was, the man with a blue blanket around his body, a saffron scarf covering his head, his gleaming skin the colour of burnt copper. Devastatingly handsome, hideously dirty.

A broken signboard caught Homi's eye. It was dangling precariously, having barely withstood a recurrent onslaught of rainstorms and heat.

M S Vaid – Palmist – Every Evening – 7 to 10.

The dim bulb hanging over the signboard blinked twice, seemingly in acknowledgement of her gaze. At once, there was a clap of thunder. Besides the address, the signboard also featured a thick arrow, pointing towards an unbelievably narrow lane. Homi peeped in – it wasn't a lane at all, just the joint entranceway to three houses.

She wasted no time in entering. Once inside, she found the same signboard hanging over the main entrance to the house on the right. The doors were wide open. The entire sitting room was the palmist's chamber. Several benches were laid out on one side of a wooden partition, behind which, she presumed, Mr Vaid examined palms in privacy. A dim light, the red oxide peeling off the floor – the dreary atmosphere of an old-fashioned homoeopathic dispensary. Lifeless.

Venturing inside, Homi found not one person waiting to have their palm read. Was the expert absent today?

She caught sight of herself in the mirror on a wall – a figure in jeans, a short kurti, an oversized leather bag. She appeared completely out of place. But her eyes blazed with curiosity, she was dying to know about herself.

Possibly her footsteps announced her presence, for

a deep voice floated across the partition.

'Come on in.'

Homi went forward.

A head of fine white hair was flying under the ceiling fan, but much more wildly than the breeze produced by that creaking machine warranted. A wind from some other source seemed to be swirling above the palmist's head. He looked old, and his clothes and steel-rimmed glasses sat awkwardly on him. Homi felt a shudder of anticipation run through her.

'I want to have my palm read,' she announced.

'Please sit down,' said Mr Vaid.

A magnifying glass, a notebook and a pencil were arranged on the large desk. There was nothing else. Drawing up a wooden chair, Homi sat down gingerly.

'Give me your hand. The right hand.'

Homi held out her hand.

'Don't you need my name, or time of birth, or anything like that, Mr Vaid?'

The man looked at her.

'The lines on your palm were formed before you were born, madam. And besides, do you think anything or anyone in the world is named correctly? A name is part of a language, isn't it?'

Mr Vaid gripped her right hand with both of

his. How hot his touch was! Homi was scalded. She leaned forward.

'What do you wish to know?' he asked.

'Tell me everything you can see or read in my palm. There's nothing specific I want to know. It's just that I've become curious about myself. I want to investigate.'

'That's all well and good, but I need questions.'

'Who am I, then, Mr Vaid?'

'You are an educated individual, self-taught – someone whose life is influenced by no one else.'

Mr Vaid sounded surprised by his own pronouncement.

'Influenced by no one else?' Homi was astonished.

'No one at all.'

'Parents, friends, lovers – none of these relationships have any influence on me?'

'As I said, the influence that most people exert is missing from your life, madam. You consider no one close or distant, good or evil. You love no one, but nor do you respect or hate them. You simply don't acknowledge the existence of others. You are the only person in your world.'

Very well.

'Here's your fate line. See, it stops almost as soon as it begins…'

'Does that mean I have no fate, Mr Vaid? Do I have no future – good or bad? No fate?'

'You have a fate. Of course you do.'

'But first tell me, do I have a man in my life?'

'You have no one in your life – not in the sense you mean.'

'No love, either?'

'No, no love. Here are the affection lines – none of them run deep. They seem to have been formed with reluctance. Your lifeline is long, but damaged. What this all tells me is that though you are currently bound in a social relationship, this bond means nothing to you. It is not a bond of love, affection or compassion. Moreover, this relationship is nearing its end.'

'What are you saying?'

Was her relationship with Lalit about to fizzle out?

'Here, look at this line. It says there is a love in your life – but that love was formed at the moment you were born. I have never seen a palm like this – never.'

Homi burst into tears.

'A love which formed at the moment I was born? Is that even possible, Mr Vaid?'

'Here's your head line. Your love has curved towards your head line, which means it is this love that will control you throughout your life.'

'Tell me more. Tell me about my successes, my enemies, good times, bad times, wealth, children, everything.'

'You have no enemies. No good or bad times. No children. Success or wealth? I cannot speak about that. They mean different things to different people.'

Homi sat in silence as Mr Vaid rattled on. Her hand lay like an inert block of wood in front of the old man.

'Your real fate line has come to a stop, madam, and a completely imagined fate line is born spontaneously at that point. It begins at the mound of imagination. Which means your future depends on how you imagine it. Your life will proceed in whatever direction you visualise it proceeding. And yet, this imagination of yours will be controlled by your fate, utterly. It's all extremely complex. Meanwhile, can you see how this very deep line emerges from the mound of Venus to bite your imagined fate line? This means that the sexuality in your life is all imagined too. The same goes for love.'

Homi didn't say a word. She couldn't.

'Your entire life is a product of your imagination, madam.'

When Homi eventually managed to find her voice, she said, 'My marriage won't last? But there's no reason for it not to. We're good friends. Lalit is a very understanding man.'

'Still, it won't last. Everything in your life is temporary.'

There was a deafening clap of thunder. The flash of lightning that preceded it was visible even deep inside the house. Finally, the rain began. A deluge, from the sound of it.

With everything she had just been told still ringing in her ears, Homi asked how much she owed for the reading. Fifty rupees – not much at all. Putting the money on the desk, she rose to her feet.

'Do you believe in fate, Mr Vaid?'

'Of course. Fate, destiny, it's all the same thing.'

'Can you tell me what fate is?'

Leaning back in his chair, the old man gave a strange laugh. He was beginning to look like a character from the epics. His lips curled downwards, while his jaw jutted out.

'fate isn't just the big things. It isn't only the sorrows and suffering, the pain and torture, the grief and accidents. Fate is every single footstep. When you wake up and yawn or stretch, that's fate too. It's predetermined. If you set off on a journey, and make it safely to the end, then that's what was predestined. If there are obstacles and delays on the way, those were predestined too. All your work, all your efforts, all your dedication only serves to take you towards your fate. No prayers, amulets, charms, or precious stones can alter your fate. This question that's occurred to you, "Who am I?", was bound to have come in just this form. And on the precise date, at the precise hour, that it did. That, too, is your fate.'

'But don't they say man is the maker of his own fate? Don't great minds say that? "As you sow, so you shall reap."'

'But those who sow do so according to their fate. They have no other choice.'

'Then, what is love?'

'Connections. Consequences. Who will meet whom, when, and in what circumstances − or will not meet at all… maybe two people have been living near each other for seven years, their lives never inter-twining, and then suddenly one day they fall in love, they develop feelings; all this is consequence. Anger, hatred, joy − all are predestined.'

A stifled scream rose from Homi's heart.

'Will I never escape my fate, Mr Vaid?'

'You are your own fate.'

Homi ran outside, straight on to the road. She saw that it was very late. Impossible to tell how late. Darkened buses and taxis were lined up on both sides of the road. The rain was soaking her through. And there, wrapped in a blanket beneath a nearby tree, stood her fate. His face was serene. As serene as though he were a true yogi. Today, there was some-thing else besides lust and depravity in his eyes. Could it be love?

The man stood there stern as a judge. In that moment, Homi fell in love with him. And realised that this was the love which had formed at the time of her birth. Exactly as the palmist had said.

The whole thing filled her with loathing.

## FATE'S ADDITION

Homi had always been a meritorious student. And a sceptic, therefore, with deep doubts about most things on earth. She accepted nothing without questioning it, although she knew full well that all questions had multiple answers. Even when she liked someone, the feeling would be laced with doubt. She questioned herself constantly regarding the appropriateness of loving or hating. And she could not subscribe fully to either faith or disbelief. Every morning, she woke up to wonder whether she had truly been asleep.

But after that day with the palmist, her life changed. As she unlocked the front door to step into her flat, exhausted by the rain, her eyes fell on the photograph of Lalit and herself on top of the fridge. And she realised that her attachment to Lalit had ended. It was over, beyond any doubt.

Lalit returned home at the break of dawn on Sunday. Homi woke up to look at him with eyes gazing at the infinite distance. Lalit didn't notice those eyes. He was barely awake. His flight from Mumbai had been delayed by a thunderstorm, finally taking off at two-thirty in the morning instead of the scheduled ten forty-five the previous night.

After changing into fresh clothes, Lalit fell into bed, while Homi got up and ate breakfast by herself. Leaving Lalit's breakfast on the table, she left for the office, though she usually had Sundays off. Walking past her colleagues' questioning eyes, Homi entered the newsroom and got down to work.

Lalit called around two-thirty.

'Where are you?'

His voice was still laced with sleep.

'At work.'

Lalit paused.

'Work? Why?'

He didn't seem to believe her. Not only was it Sunday, he had just got home after a ten-day business trip. Why was Homi at the office?

'When will you be back?' he demanded, clearly irked. He no longer sounded sleepy.

'After visiting Baba', Homi answered.

'What's happened to you, Khuku?'

'Nothing. Why do you ask?'

'How's uncle?'

'Stable, but no improvement.'

'I'm sorry I haven't been able to check in the last couple of days, Khuku. Have they said how much longer he needs to be in hospital?'

'No, but there's no question of discharging him now.'

'Are you angry because I fell asleep without kissing you, Khuku?'

'Not at all. Relax.'

'I wish you hadn't gone to work today.'

'You always say that, Lalit. It's pointless. I have to go to work if there's work to be done. Don't you do the same? How can you demand I stay at home?'

Suhash, working next to Homi, turned to glance at her as her voice became louder.

'Demand?' Lalit echoed.

'Ok.'

He hung up.

When Homi got to the hospital that evening she found her mother there, calculating how much had been spent so far, and how much more would be needed. Homi waited for the doctor. There was no point going in to see her father. It was the doctor she needed to talk to.

'What's the problem, Ma?' she said.

'Just keep using whatever money Baba's put away.'

'And when that runs out? Do you know what the bill will eventually come to, Khuku?'

'I know it'll be high. Very high. It's about fifteen thousand a day at the moment.'

'Well then! Have you any idea how much liquid cash we have left?'

'You've never told me.'

'Have you asked? Have you ever even bothered to ask?'

Homi abruptly decided to have some fun at her mother's expense.

'Sell the house, if it comes that. Kejriwal has made a huge offer.'

'How dare you!' Homi's mother screamed in the centre of the crowded lounge. 'It's my father's house. I was born there. I will never sell it.'

'Look, Ma, you'll have to make your own decisions about money. It's entirely up to you, there's nothing I can do about it. What I can do, if you want me to, is have Baba transferred to a cheaper hospital, or even have him taken home.'

Homi's mother scanned her from head to toe, then delivered her verdict.

'Go ahead. He'll survive if he's meant to survive.'

She had gone home by the time Homi emerged from her meeting with the doctor. The religious rites after Mr Banerjee's death were to be performed the following day. But Oli and his family were on a collision course, with the result that none of them were willing to be in each other's presence. So Oli had turned to Mrs Banerjee, telling her mother that she at least must be there.

'How can rites like these be observed without the family elders?' Homi's mother had told her.

'That's why I told Oli her aunts won't be there, they have nothing to gain.'

So she would be at Sunny Park tomorrow morning for the ritual.

But Homi wasn't worried about her mother or Oli. She had never let herself be worried about them. Instead, she was thinking about the fact that Lalit had not called since their last strained conversation. She had been expecting to see him waiting for her outside the hospital – that would have been the most natural response. He had always drawn on his warmth and love to absorb all her anger, her obstinacy and hurt. He had never rubbed it in when she had been wrong. Today, too, she had been sure that Lalit would be there, trying to catch her eye, insisting that they go somewhere together.

Whether or not she was still in love with him, she had really needed this. Just this small gesture.

Homi went home with Lalit on her mind. Unlocking the front door, she entered to find the flat in darkness. So Lalit wasn't home.

Switching on the dim light in the drawing room, she sat down on the sofa. Had she been hoping that he would be waiting for her here, perhaps bursting with rage, or sullen with resentment?

She sat there for a long time before finally calling him. But there was no answer. Where was he? Was he with his friends? At a pub or nightclub? Was he drinking somewhere?

Homi's heart twisted suddenly. She felt a stab of fear – fear of losing Lalit. Even if she didn't love him, she told herself, she could still be afraid of losing him.

Homi called him again, and once more the dial tone ran through to the end.

And again, with the same result.

A compulsion seized hold of Homi, and she began to call Lalit over and over, seventeen or eighteen times in all. Lalit, her husband, her only friend in the world, a man of whom she had once demanded that they stay in touch every moment, to which he had agreed – it was him that Homi began to look for madly over the phone network. Once, she had actually gone directly to Lalit's office all because he hadn't taken her call. Lalit had been in a meeting, so Homi sat sobbing in his cubicle. He'd been dumbfounded when he returned and found her there.

'What's going on? Everyone's been telling me, "Your girlfriend's here, crying her eyes out". What's wrong?'

'Why didn't you take my call?'

'I was in a meeting, baby.'

'I thought you'd left me, that I'd never see you again.'

'So you came here crying? You crazy girl. All right, in future I'll let you know when I won't be able to take your call. At least, I'll try. But if it happens again, just don't panic.'

Glancing out through the glass wall of his cubicle, he said,

'Look at them, they're all wondering what's going on.'

He touched her cheek.

'But I loved it. Silly girl.'

She had wiped her tears away and was getting up to go when Lalit stopped her.

'How can I let you go off alone now?' he had said. 'Let's both of us get out of here.'

Homi tried calling Lalit one last time, and, bringing all her trauma to an end, he answered.

'Yes, what is it?'

He seemed in a tremendous hurry, which made Homi hesitate before asking her own question.

'Where are you?'

'New Alipur, with Ma.'

Lalit said this in a way that suggested he was back in his own space, as though he had never developed any sort of relationship with this 12,000-rupees-a-month flat in Hindustan Park. Could a flat become a home for two people from different places purely because they lived there together?

All of a sudden, Homi felt rootless.

'When will you be back?' she asked.

'Not tonight. It's Sonu's birthday. My aunts are here, so's Rinki. Lots of people. I'll need to go straight to the office tomorrow.'

Sonu, Sonia, was Lalit's brother's daughter.

'This isn't fair, Lalit,' Homi told him.

'It isn't? Really? All right, Khuku, I'll talk to you later. They're waiting for me, we were in the middle of eating.'

Lalit hung up. And for the first time, it occurred to Homi that the way he had treated her just then was exactly how she had treated him for the past year and a half.

*This isn't fair, Lalit.*

She had never spoken to him that way before, had she? She'd been stubborn, and had proven incapable of shouldering responsibilities, but never devoid of feeling. And because she had never been indifferent or hostile, Lalit had not felt deprived. She had considered Lalit extremely caring. But the truth was that today she had been paid back in the same coin. And his undisguised rejection had changed the picture entirely.

# SCRIPT AND SCRIPTURE

As decreed by fate, Homi had met Lalit for the first
time on the landing of the office staircase. It was
December, and the city was going through a particularly cold spell. Evening was descending, the sky
occupied by birds eager to return to their nests. Homi
was gazing at them through the glass windows which
surrounded the staircase. A little while ago she had
broken up with Rudra, and she was trying to fill the
empty space with a solitude that did not hurt.

If she looked down at the office compound,
she would see a succession of cars hurtling in, with
reporters leaping out of them. The rush peaked at 5
PM, as everyone got ready for the 6 PM bulletin, the 7
PM sports round-up and the 8 PM metro news. People
ran around either barking instructions or hurrying to
respond to them. When Homi did look down, she saw
a famous footballer getting out of a car, presumably a
guest for a panel discussion. The very next moment

she saw an actor walking up the stairs, removing his sunglasses.

Homi had meant to go out for a smoke. She enjoyed shivering in the cold, as she was now. She kept touching her cheek in a way that made it clear she was lonely, very lonely at that moment. And Lalit, the young but dynamic and successful Lalit Basu, an executive at the large banking corporation which handled all the financial affairs of the media conglomerate where Homi was employed, had just come out of a meeting with Vipul Mehta from Administration, racing down the stairs towards the landing, where Homi stood with a lit cigarette she wasn't smoking, gazing wistfully at the sky.

Had Lalit not seen Homi that afternoon, and in that particular context; had he walked down the granite steps still in conversation with Vipul Mehta, and never looked at her at all; and had it not still been winter the next time he went to her office, had she not been peering intently at her computer screen when she did, on a hectic day, signalling her loneliness in the midst of the hectic office, would Lalit still have been curious about her? Would the image have registered strongly enough for him to have remembered her instantly at the company party a month later? Would it still have ensured that he never lost sight of her, not even for a moment in that crowded room? On the dance floor, they had come face to face. It was Lalit who had refilled her empty wine glass. And then the table at which Homi sat down, exhausted after dancing, also had Lalit sitting at it, along with several others with whom he had been talking and laughing, an exuberant circle he drew her into. They had spent the next three hours together, eating their dinner together as well. All the red wine on an empty stomach gave Homi heartburn. She had felt like vomiting during dinner, but the desserts were delicious, so she had tried to suppress her nausea.

She remembered Lalit offering to drive her home, and that she had got out of the car at midnight, opposite Victoria Memorial, to throw up generously into the road.

Lalit had offered his handkerchief, and bought her a bottle of cola.

'How about some fresh air?' he had suggested.

They had spent the rest of the night wandering around Victoria Memorial, the Maidan and Fort William. She had told him about herself, and also about Rudra. He told her about Paroma, the girl he had grown close to at business school. He had played some delectable music for her on the car stereo before turning to Homi and announcing, 'I don't have a girlfriend right now, but I'm looking.'

'What kind of girl do you like?' she had asked.

'Someone with a sense of humour. I'm not fond of girls who take life too seriously. Someone who does everything according to plan is not my cup of tea. What about you – what sort of boy do you like? Or are you hoping to get back together with Rudra?'

Both of them had dropped enough hints to suggest they had begun to like each other. The roadside tea shop next to the Sikh temple by P.G. Hospital had just opened. Homi and Lalit drunk tea from large earthen pots, then he drove her to Belvedere Road. They had met again that evening in a Theatre Road cafe. After this, they began to meet every day, call each other constantly, and chat all night on the phone. Those conversations were so full of promise, those dates and long drives so irresistible, that love soon arrived, with a relationship hot on its heels. Their love affair generated enough heat to melt steel. Theirs was a blind desire, a primordial and unadulterated physical need. As soon as she got into his car they would wind up the windows, turn on the air-conditioning and begin to kiss, their kisses falling everywhere they could reach, tilting their seats back so that they could have oral sex. Finally, they had met in an empty flat belonging to one of Lalit's bachelor friends for a screaming climax.

They had actually crashed from the bed to the floor in the middle of fucking, but neither had noticed any pain. Homi had held Lalit's head to her breast, for she knew that the head played an important role in sex. Lalit's head had seemed on the heavy side to her, and this was something to savour. Homi had been extremely relieved to find that his head was shapely.

Tonight, in this darkened flat, the fatalism that overcame Homi convinced her that their love affair, and all her previous affairs, had been utterly controlled by fate. But be that as it may, it was still Lalit whom she had loved the most till now, Lalit she had mistrusted the least. She could tell that it would take her some time to forget him. But the chain of events was unfolding without pause, just as it was fated to. It could not be stopped by any means – or so the palmist had told her. In any case, she could sense Lalit retreating, establishing a distance between them. There was no wound, no bleeding, no injury to the flesh of her heart – and yet Lalit was pulling away from her. Taking the form of a python – enormous and grotesque – fate was swallowing her, and Lalit too.

# CREATING FATE

That Monday, Homi and Lalit's sole interaction consisted of a terse conversation about a credit card payment. After meeting with the doctor, Homi left the hospital to track down a few medicines. Her father had developed a strange rash, so the visiting doctor, Dr Jalan, had changed all the prescriptions. It was 9 PM by the time she had bought them, returned, and handed them over to the nurse.

When she got back to Hindustan Park, Homi didn't bother to ring the bell. She didn't even want to wonder whether Lalit was home or not. Entering, she found the lamp on in the bedroom and the TV running. Lalit was lying back in bed, working on his laptop with great concentration. A bottle of whisky, a half-filled glass, and a plate with remnants of onions, tomatoes and mustard sauce crowded the bedside table. The crumbs suggested fish cutlets or something similar. So he'd eaten without waiting for her.

In the bedroom, Homi took off her clothes one by one, until she was fully naked, but still Lalit didn't look up from his computer. She was wondering how to start up a conversation. About to head into the bathroom for a shower, she stopped and spoke instead.

'I thought you wouldn't come back.'

Lalit finally raised his eyes, flying into an instant rage.

'You thought? Well, that's a first. What's your problem, Khuku? Why can't you change your ways?'

'Like how?' said Homi.

'I always see your mother in you.'

'Lalit!'

Now Homi was equally furious.

'It's true. But get this into your head: I will never become your father. Don't expect you can body-slam me to the floor whenever you feel like it. You ought to take a long, hard look at yourself. You want to be some unhinged intellectual? I've seen plenty of them, ok. I'll tell you what, I'm beginning to think love is actually hatred. When a man loves a woman like you, when he gives up everything else, he begins to hate himself. His self-respect vanishes. Which is exactly what is happening to me, damn it.'

'Don't take me for a fool, Lalit,' Homi spat back. 'I never cared for the smell of your love. You always had this aura of kindness, as though I was some sickly patient you were looking after. You're calling me unhinged? How dare you?'

'Oh, you'll never be a real mad woman. And as for kindness, who's going to be kind to someone like you? You people are the one showering us with charity.'

'People like you! People like you!'

Homi spun on her heel and slapped Lalit.

His expression darkened instantly. He dragged Homi to the bed, flung her down on it, took off his clothes, twisted her hair to pull her head back, and forced her thighs apart with his knee. Homi realised that it was not clear what fate really wanted, copulation or separation. Which of them was spontaneous, and which only came with effort? Their relationship was now balanced on a knife edge.

'Let me go, Lalit,' she wailed. 'Please let me go. Don't do this to me. Don't humiliate me like this. Shame on you!'

Lalit let go of her at once. Another of those meaningless arguments which usually led to a fortnight without sex. Lalit went to the bathroom. Homi crawled under the covers and drew her knees up to her chest.

Seven or eight days afterwards, Lalit woke Homi

up to ask, 'Tell me, Khuku, have you fallen in love with someone? Tell me the truth, or I won't be able to sleep.'

'Love, sex, friendship – I don't need those things anymore,' she answered.

# SEQUENTIALLY

'Listen Khuku, Arati is plain blackmailing me.'

Mrs Banerjee wasted no time on niceties.

Homi couldn't remember the last time she had entered her father's room. Possibly on the day of her marriage, when she had stood at his door holding Lalit's hand after their private registered wedding. Mr Dutta's stooping figure had approached the pair, hitching up his pyjamas as he did so.

'What is it?'

That day, too, Homi had noticed the dirty mosquito net strung up in his room. It was still there today.

'This is Lalit, Baba,' she had told him. 'We were friends earlier. We're husband and wife now. We came to pay our respects.'

He had nodded twice, standing with his hands on his hips, but his gaze never strayed higher than Lalit's feet.

'Go along inside,' he had said.

Homi had brought along a washerman from the railway quarters. One by one, she began to take down the mosquito net, bedclothes, curtains, and table-cloth, all of which had been in use for at least twenty years, for all she knew without ever being laundered. When she stripped the cover off the pillow, cotton balls burst out of the casing and rolled all over the floor.

Her mother was still in full flow.

'She joined in a flash when I told her the pay was a thousand. It's gone up to two thousand now. Then, when I told her your father's coming home, she said she won't do it for less than three thousand. The nerve of her! Oh, she's a real bitch. I haven't seen too many women as greedy as her.'

Homi had to step around her mother to get out of her father's room. In the dining room, the ornamental posts on either side of the huge wooden crockery cab-inet had hooks on them, from which hung all sorts of keys. Homi located the key to her second-floor room, went up and unlocked the door. She was entering her room for the first time in over a year. Ignoring its musty smell, she opened the drawer beneath the bed to retrieve some bedding. She left the room, lock-ing the door behind her, and carried it downstairs. With the rainy season still ongoing, everything had an odour of damp. Homi tried to air out the bedclothes before making her father's bed.

'Do you have any naphthalene, Ma?'

'Plenty, Khuku,' Mrs Banerjee said, without making any motion to fetch some … 'You could have bought one of those mops on a stick, you know, they're the easiest to use.'

'I will,' Homi said.

The washerman took the old bedclothes away, saying, 'How can I wash these? They'll split the moment I touch them.'

Homi's father was coming back from the hospital that day, after nearly a month and a half. At the hospital, Dr Jalan had drawn Homi aside.

'Look, your father has lived his life and he's not going to get a second chance. It's just a matter of how long he can keep breathing. He's not responding to treatment, so there's no point keeping him here. Take him home.'

Her mother had no objection. Two caregivers and two nurses would divide each day between them. Homi had made arrangements for oxygen cylinders, too. Dr Jalan had warned her not to let her father develop bedsores, but as everyone knew, for someone whose movement was reduced to opening and closing their eyes, certain things were unavoidable. Sores, bugs, blood, pus, stench – and finally death.

Homi's mother was strangely calm about the whole affair. She hadn't even mentioned Mr Dutta once. When Homi was almost done getting the room ready, her mother offered her a cup of tea.

'What do you want for lunch, Khuku?'

Homi sipped her tea.

'Nothing, I'm going back to work now. I'll be at the hospital at four.'

Her mother drew up a chair to sit down facing her.

'It's time to replace the fridge, Khuku. We can't go on with such an old machine. Everything that goes in freezes over, there's so much ice I can't even tell what's in there. Arati got some fish three or four days ago, but I don't remember whether I ate it or not. Not that I'm going to ask her to get me anything ever again. You have no idea how she cheats me. She claimed she paid a hundred and fifty for that fish. Daylight robbery! She'll steal every rupee I have. I must get a replacement. And, Khuku, about the fridge… you really must get me a new one. Oli was very upset, *"Replace the fridge, replace the TV, replace the air-conditioner,"* she told me. Apparently she doesn't even like the sound of the doorbell. So I told her, why don't you get it done? The house belongs to you, too. And that man who was such a burden on you, he's gone now. It's time you did something for your mother. What did I get? Dead silence. Well, silence and tears. Apparently she was missing her children.'

Homi sighed.

'I should go, Ma. The nurse will be here at four, her name is Sulekha. Show her where everything is.'

Her mother paid no attention.

'I'd made some hilsa. And it reminded Oli of her children. *"They spent their entire childhoods at boarding school, then my son went to the US when he grew up, my daughter to Italy, I've never been able to cook a meal for them. Aniruddha loves hilsa so much ..."* You should have heard her wailing. She let them grow up away from her because she didn't want the burden of having them around, and now she can't stop thinking of them? And of course, she has all the time in the world to weep for her children, but when it comes to her mother, oh no, it's never convenient. Although I mustn't lie, she did bring me the walking shoes this time. But do you know what she said after giving them to me?'

Mrs Banerjee was gasping for breath.

' *"Hand the house over to property developers, Ma, what good is this white elephant, get a three-bedroom flat."* I told her to her face, Khuku, that it will never happen. I was born in this house, and I will die here. 'It's for your own good that I'm telling you,' she said. So I told her, "You don't have to worry about what's good for me, Oli, think about what's good for you." At that, you know, Khuku, she became very angry. *"Stop it, Ma, stop it. You've got a twisted mind, you're always look-ing for some ulterior motive."* You tell me, Khuku, how can I possibly move to a flat at my age? None of you has any idea, a crow drowned in the water-tank, do you know how difficult it was to find someone to clean it up? I can barely manage such crises, but who else is there for me to rely on? When I can't do things for myself anymore, when I become a cripple like your father, it'll be up to you. Or maybe you'll just throw me out on the streets.'

Sighing over this storm of tears, Homi gave her a mother a light hug.

'Don't fret so much Ma, just leave it to fate.'

'Are you telling me your kind believes in fate?'

Trailing Homi down the stairs to the front entrance, Mrs Banerjee recalled another complaint.

'When are you taking me to the dentist, Khuku? I can't chew with this side of my mouth. I gave away the food to Arati, it was getting stale anyway. Oh, she got it all.'

In the street outside the house, Homi hailed a taxi.

Just as it pulled up, another woman of a similar age ran up and jumped in.

'But this is my taxi!' Homi exclaimed – then she recognised the intruder. It was Bonnie, Rudra's former classmate, someone she had known quite well.

Bonnie had recognised her too, and smiled.

'Oh, hi, Homi. Jump in.'

Homi shrugged.

'I'm going to AJC Bose Road.'

'Same route, I'm going to Nightingale.'

As she got in, Homi realised that Bonnie was sizing her up.

'So, how are things with you?' Bonnie asked.

'All ok. How about you?'

'I'm studying for an M.D.. Began this year. You know Rudra's studying for an M.S., right?'

'No, I didn't, and there's no reason I should.'

There was a traffic jam outside the zoo. The taxi was motionless. The longer the journey, the longer the conversation would be.

'Rudra was so in love with you once,' Bonnie threw in, 'but he's very critical now.'

It was the way Bonnie said it – Homi had no choice but to ask.

'How do you mean?'

'We were talking about you just the other day. I

was the one who brought the subject up. Sometimes you feel nostalgic for no particular reason. I was thinking of all us getting together, of you and Rudra being in love. The picnic on the roof of his house. You and Rudra had already tasted blood by then, but all I was doing was plucking at my pimples. Anyway, we were reminiscing about those times when Rudra made this really offensive comment about you.'

'Oh?'

Was Bonnie seeking revenge for the way she had suffered during Rudra and Homi's affair?

'You know what he said? Apparently he'd been very depressed after the two of you broke up; he had even thought of suicide. But gradually he realised how much things improved for him after you left him. He claimed you were ruining his future. He couldn't focus on his studies because you wouldn't let him go to class, and forced him to spend the day with you. He said you'd drag him to mysterious dark places beneath trees, that you clung to him, suffocated him. He was only mad about you because you were so beautiful – as a person, there was nothing to love, he said. Apparently you're the most self-centred woman he's ever met.'

'What else?'

'That you always wanted him entirely to yourself,

you took him away from all his friends. So it was just you and him, all the time. He said you were a bore. Sick, even.'

The taxi was passing PG Hospital.

'No relationship lasts forever, Bonnie,' Homi said. 'They're all bound to break down for one reason or another. Those were definitely the reasons in our case, mine and Rudra's. I can't say it makes me happy to hear all this, but it's true, that's what I'm like.'

She slipped out in front of the Exide building, making an excuse about one-way traffic regulations, and took a different taxi.

As she was about to enter her office, Homi ran into Gouri, who was rushing in followed by Richard the cameraman. They must have been on a shoot. Gouri was struggling to contain her excitement, the picture of a journalist who's just landed a scoop.

'What have you got, Gouri?' Homi asked as they walked upstairs.

'A sensational story, Homi. A woman named Meena, her husband died of diarrhoea just three days ago. Meena is six months pregnant. She's decided not to keep the baby now that her husband is dead. She wants an abortion. But an abortion at six months is impossible.'

In the newsroom, Yash came up to them.

'How's the situation?'

'It's a mess, Yash,' said Gouri.

'Just give it a quick edit and put it on air.'

'So what happened?' Homi asked after Yash had left.

'What do you think?' Gouri continued hurriedly.

'The more the doctor tried to explain, the more she pleaded, insisting that she doesn't want to keep the baby, she wants it taken out. The doctor told her, *"It's a crime, it's murder, the police will arrest you, and me too."* Who's going to make her understand? Foetuses are killed all the time.'

Gouri rushed off to her desk, leaving Homi to mull the story over. She went looking for Yash, finally tracking him down in the conference room.

'Is your story on single mothers finished?' Yash asked her.

'I just need one more day. But the promo starts tomorrow. You haven't seen it?'

He had.

'Add in some more sound bites from single mother celebrities,' he told her. 'The story should reflect how tough it really is, that it's a big challenge to bring up a child single-handed.'

'I don't think it is all that challenging anymore, Yash. There are plenty of single mothers these days.

And all of them are managing their careers quite effectively, at the same time as raising their children …'

'Are you saying the struggles of single mothers are a thing of the past?'

'Watch the story, Yash, listen to the interviews. The only thing everyone talks about is time management. A structured routine is all they need.'

'Well, so society is changing. This is the kind of new outlook we want to present. Keep it up! Your team's doing great work, Homi.'

'Oh yes, they really are. But there's something I was just wondering, Yash. Up to which stage is abortion legal? At what point does it become murder? When does a foetus begin to be acknowledged as a human being? Don't you think these questions are inevitable, in the context of Gouri's story?'

Yash thought for a few minutes.

'Can you call Pritha?' he said.

Pritha arrived, and soon they had set up a panel discussion on the subject to take place at 9 PM. But Homi was still clearly deep in thought.

'What else, Homi?' Yash asked her.

'I'm thinking, this is only one side of the story. The other side is, it's my body, I'm carrying something in it. How far do my rights as an independent human being go in deciding whether to carry a baby or not? If I can choose to keep it, why can't I also choose to get rid of it?'

'You mean, what rights does Meena have in this case?'

'What rights does a human being actually have over themselves? At what point is my body or mind taken over by the state? When does the state or society get to decide what should be done with my body or my mind, and therefore decree what I can or cannot do?'

'Too complicated, Homi,' Pritha shook her head. 'Too much nuance.'

'We'll work on this later, Homi, all right?' Yash's expression suggested that he genuinely understood Homi's concern and would give the matter sufficient attention as soon as he had the time.

Homi left the office just before 6 PM. She hadn't even told Lalit that this was the day she was taking her father back home. She would have to do everything by herself. Though it had been this way for some time now. These days, Lalit and Homi avoided each other. They ate their meals separately, not at home. They still slept, exhausted, in the same bed, but no different from how people slept in long-distance trains, practically side by side. It didn't mean there was any intimacy involved.

Leaving Belvedere Road around 9:30 PM after installing her father in his home, Homi wondered whether she really needed to go back to Hindustan Park.

'What's going on Khuku, how come you're doing everything all by yourself?' her mother had asked. 'I don't see Lalit anywhere these days. He hasn't called, either. Anything wrong?'

'It's not working, Ma,' Homi had told her. 'I haven't spoken to Lalit about it yet, but I might have to make a decision very soon.'

Her mother had raised her eyebrows.

'So quickly? Should I get your room cleaned, then? The mattress has rotted, mind you.'

About to say she would have it cleaned if necessary, Homi simply said no instead.

Back home, she discovered that the flat looked like it had been ransacked. Lalit's papers, books, files, and shoes were scattered everywhere. None of her own things was among them. But her zipped bundles of expensive saris and winter clothes were piled on one side of the bed. It was as though Lalit had been forced to take her clothes out but not really wanted to touch them. As soon as she entered the bedroom, Lalit took her hand and made her sit down on the bed. His eyes were glittering, but there was neither anger, loathing nor frustrated desire in his expression. He reached under the pillow and pulled out a stamped deed.

'This is the lease for the flat, Khuku. I've spoken to the landlord, he will transfer it to you. The rent is unchanged. It's no problem if you don't want to transfer it just yet, the agreement still has more than a year to go.'

'Are you leaving, Lalit?'

'I have no choice, Khuku.'

'Where will you go?'

'You know the company's been asking me to move to Bangalore. I was holding out mainly for you. But when a woman has no further need for love, sex or friendship, continuing to live with her is demeaning. After all, I'm a man. I may not be able to possess you, but there are still certain requirements. When it comes to relationships, I'm afraid I have many demands. You're making a mistake if you consider me anything like your father. Don't mind my saying this, every-one loves themselves to some extent, but too much of self-love is not good. Honestly, Khuku, even your eyes have changed. Just the other night I woke up to the sound of you crying – you were on the balcony, there was a huge moon, a full moon, it must have been. You were gazing up at it and weeping, saying something I couldn't make out. I got frightened and called out to you. You looked at me, but you didn't recognise me. Your eyes that night, they were a mad-woman's eyes.'

Lalit continued after a pause.

'I can't deal with you, Khuku. Your self-love will destroy you one day.'

Homi considered telling Lalit, 'You're right – the palmist called it a love that formed the moment I was born. I didn't understand him, then.'

Instead, she said, 'What will I do with this flat? I can't afford it on my own. How much will I have left over, after paying twelve thousand out of twenty-four as rent?'

'You want to go back to Belvedere Road?'

'No, I don't.'

'Then keep the flat, I'll pay my half of the rent.'

'Why? Why should you?'

Lalit took Homi's face in his hands.

'Because I'm the one running away.'

At this, Homi burst out laughing.

'You fool, Lalit!'

The letter came on the afternoon about twenty days after Lalit had left Kolkata, the day she had taken leave from her office to move house. It was a draft document for mutual divorce, accompanied by a brief personal note.

*You're a sceptic, Khuku, you're very philosophical. I respect you, but I cannot be as indifferent as you are about your own and other people's lives. No matter what, I have roots: I have a past, a present, a future. Make up your mind, quickly. If nothing else, I miss your friendship. Love, Lalit.*

Sitting down with the letter, Homi searched her own spaces of love, friendship, and desire, with a fine-tooth comb. But instead of finding anything, she discovered that the event she had been contemplating had already fully taken place.

## TIME AND THE
## MESSENGER OF FATE

Homi had come to rely on fate controlling the sequence of events in her life – and not only matters of the heart. Her material circumstances were also undergoing a dramatic transformation. She left the Hindustan Park flat and moved into an old building in nearby Gariahat. It was situated next to a well-known sari store. There were shops selling jewellery and crockery on the ground floor. There was even a kiosk for cigarettes and soft drinks, leading an uncertain existence. After the building's original owner had died, the potential inheritors had started wrangling with one another over the property, and one of them had taken advantage of the dispute to convert the portion under their control – part of the first floor – into a boarding house for women. There was a small dining room near the entrance. The first room on the right was a shared living room, beside which there were two large bedrooms with en suite bathrooms. Each of these rooms held four people, but the space was large enough for it not to feel crowded.

Homi fell in love with the house at first sight. High ceilings with rafters, subtle mosaic patterns on the floor, thick walls, long slatted windows that ran all the way down to the floor. The long balcony running outside the rooms was suspended over a pavement. This being Gariahat, a hundred different trades went on beneath it, and thousands of people passed by in a noisy crush. Every evening neon advertisements flashed a few inches from the women's noses. After the lights went out at night, the neon signs continued blinking, casting their glow onto the women's sleeping bodies, making them look like fairies. A red beam intermittently illuminated Homi's bed. Gazing at its source, she was filled with delight at the thought that no one she knew was aware of her new address. She felt that now, she really did belong nowhere, a condition that had gained material existence in the world, beyond its origin in the faint lines on her palms.

Immediately after moving house, Homi had taken a week's leave from work. There was a rush every morning, with the boarding house emptying out by 10 AM, and then she was left alone in her new space till evening. She spent the afternoon lying in bed with a book or walking around the house. It was difficult to spend much time on the balcony, because so many electric and phone cables ran through it. And then, every evening just before darkness fell, its neon advertisements came to life, after which it was impossible to venture out there.

The drawing room consisted of an old carpet, a dilapidated sofa, and an ancient radiogram. This was where the boarders met their guests, offering them tea in cups balanced on a wooden stool.

Homi observed the other women closely. They all seemed quite well-off, and all were busy with their respective jobs. They each paid 4,000 rupees a month, which also covered the service of a cook and a maid. Two thousand out of the four was the rent, while the remaining two thousand went towards food, cooking gas, electricity, the cook and maid's salaries, and maintenance of the boarding house. The responsibility for running the place rotated between the boarders.

One of the women was a medical representative, another, a dancer in a troupe which travelled the world and featured a well-known actress. One of them single-handedly ran a dealership for a foreign cosmetics brand. Ratnaboli in the next room was a college professor, while Sharmila was a homoeopathic doctor, with a position in a hospital. Khushi was an up-and-coming model. Some of them were married, some divorced. Khushi had a boyfriend, with whom she chatted till three in the morning in a voice softer than breath.

Homi had never before got to know the kind of women she now lived with – ordinary middle-class people, cultured and courteous. Earning and spending money played an important role in their lives. They often got into a celebratory mood, which was when they bought chicken, cooked it with hot spices, and ate it with steaming rice on their beds, hoisting their floppy gowns above their knees. The next morning they were off to work again. Khushi was the liveliest of them all, chattering all the time. She showed everyone whatever new thing she bought, even underclothes.

'We were missing a journalist,' she had told Homi on her first day in the boarding house.

The next day, reclining on Homi's bed, she had asked, 'What's the matter with you? Why are you in bed all the time? Is it depression?'

'I just wanted to rest for a few days,' Homi had explained.

'Where did you live before?'

Khushi had taken a cigarette from Homi's pack without asking.

'Hindustan Park.'

'Oh, that's close by. What was the boarding house like? Or were you a paying guest?'

'It was great, I really liked it.'

'And what about your family home?'

It was a question Homi hadn't known how to answer. She had looked in silence at Khushi, who must have drawn her own conclusions as she jumped up, saying, 'Sharmila's calling me, let me see what she wants.'

After a lazy morning and afternoon, Homi would – though purely out of obligation – go to Belvedere Road to visit her father, then return to her boarding room.

When the week was over and she went back to work, her shift had changed.

'Did you see Dr Dutta before going on leave, Homi?' Yash asked her.

Dr Dutta was the medical officer at the office. It was compulsory to see him for a check-up every two months. Homi confirmed that she had.

'The thing is,' Yash said, 'he's saying that your mental condition is precarious. That you're in distress. And so it wouldn't be right for you to be under too much pressure at work. You probably wouldn't be able to meet the company's needs, either. And yet, we're close to Durga Puja, you can imagine the situation. Everyone's having to give 110%. So we've decided to put you on the night shift for a couple of months. Your department's pretty quiet at night, so you can take it easy – do a little work, chat with the others. You can even skip coming in from time to time. We need you to get back to your old self, physically and mentally. We need the old Homi. New ideas, big smiles!'

So Homi's afternoons continued to be spent in bed. Her shift began at 10 PM, which meant she didn't have to take a taxi till 9:30. Sometimes there wasn't even a free desk. Smita, who used to be her assistant, was now responsible for the entire day's work. She barely had time to look up from her screen. Only after Smita had left could Homi sit down at a computer. Smita even left instructions for her every night.

'Don't open the files directly, Homi, drag them onto the desktop to make new ones. Or else you know what'll happen.'

Smita looked at her as though trying to gauge whether Homi remembered these things.

It was true that Homi had grown forgetful these days. Sometimes she felt like there was only some superficial information floating around inside her head, and even this seemed to sink out of sight most of the time. Then some of it would pop up again. If the correct information floated up at the appropriate moment, she could produce a convincing response.

'I know, the system will crash.'

'Please, Homi, don't mess it up.'

No, she didn't mess anything up. She just sat there gazing at the computer screen while the office emptied out. All the conversations, all the decibels climbed to a crescendo, then, at midnight, began to fade. The last newsreader didn't even have the patience to take off her make-up. The young men from the catering company finished stacking the plates, bowls and glasses, and left. The bright lights in the cafeteria and corridors were dimmed. The conference rooms were locked. The teenage boy in charge of dispensing coffee and snacks lay down in a corner of the cafeteria, but couldn't get any sleep, as there was always someone or other demanding coffee.

The newsroom grew busy again at 2:30 AM. With the approach of dawn, stories began to be written, edited and aired – everyone's life acquired the inevitable momentum of office work. The night reporter led a tormented existence, with constant calls to the police headquarters and fire-brigade: 'Any accidents? Any fires?'

Homi went to the cafeteria. The lights were

turned down, the air-conditioning a near-silent hum. She pulled out a chair to sit down, and the boy sat up at the sound.

'Coffee, Didi?'

'I'm fine,' she said, 'go back to sleep.'

He closed his eyes again immediately. Homi's gaze travelled beyond the glass windows to an almost-deserted AJC Bose Road. Trucks shattered the night from time to time, roaring along the road. At those moments, Homi realised she had no work anymore, no duties, no plans, no enquiries to be made – everything had been resolved. She also realised that, even if the need for love, sex, and friendship ends, certain bonds remain. And so, she had to keep sitting there. She had to remain awake.

And she did remain awake, playing a game of shadows with herself – while, very close by, only on the other side of the road, her fate stood sleepless beneath a huge tree with dense foliage, gazing at her with steadfast eyes. How eternally his love for her pulsed! Homi locked eyes with her own fate, hypnotised.

Gradually, she began to see the young hermit everywhere, at all hours. Standing with his palms pressed together at his chest, on the street opposite the boarding house; just in front of her, descending the stairs to the metro station; following her on the pavement of Theatre Road. His blanket trailed behind him, sweeping the ground, while his expression revealed his single-minded focus – that his mind was filled with Homi.

Durga Puja was here. Lalit returned to Kolkata, called her and asked to meet. She agreed – she felt a deep urge to meet him after all this time, practically a sensation of joy. It seemed to her that even if there was no love, it was impossible to obliterate the weakness that she had discovered in herself, that she had allocated to herself. Desire faded, but didn't disappear entirely. Even as everything was swept out of her heart and mind, the agony of loss remained. It was a peculiar script to have to follow.

They met at the coffee shop of a five-star hotel on the night the idols were taken for immersion in the river. It was Homi who had suggested the location, because she would have to go to Belvedere Road afterwards with some medicine and food for her father.

'What have you done to yourself, Khuku?' Lalit asked as soon as he saw her. 'Why the dark circles?'

He shook his head in violent disapproval, taking her hands in both of his.

'What did you gain by pushing me away?

'It's all very well to be impulsive, obstinate, unpredictable, et cetera, but you built this relationship too, didn't you? It was your relationship too, wasn't it? Couldn't you have considered for even a moment that you'd lose me? The first time I met you, Khuku, I was attracted by your romanticism. Then I realised you don't live in the real world. You feel neither anger nor affection. And yet, you are vengeful.

'Do you remember what happened at the Lake Gardens Southern Avenue crossing, Khuku? When we parked at the signal, this little beggar boy came up the window, saying *give me some money, Didi, for food*. You sighed but didn't give him anything. The boy tried twice more, then moved away and said, *one slap, you bitch*. At once, you took a ten-rupee note out of your bag, the boy was already at the window of another car, but you called him back. You weren't smiling, but there was no anger in your expression either. The boy came running when he saw the money. And the red light turned to green. As soon as the boy came up to the window, you said, *one kick in your balls, you bastard*.

'I don't think I understood you at all, Khuku. Let me know if your zest for life ever returns – it'll make me very happy to know.'

Lalit left a small package for her, containing lipstick, perfume, shower gel, and a Japanese fan. Homi distributed these gifts among the other boarders.

—

One night, just after 1 AM, the lines began to buzz with news from Mumbai. 'Abu Salem arrested in Portugal. Monica Bedi and Abu Salem to be flown to Mumbai by this evening.' Homi got goosebumps. For the first time in a long while, she felt the blood coursing through her frozen limbs.

Growing restless, she called Yash, told the librarian to pull footage of the Mumbai bomb blasts from the archives, and to collect all the stories done so far on Dawood Ibrahim's D Company.

'Put it on Breaking News!' she shouted.

Seeing how worked up she was, Pradyumna said,

'Calm down, Homi. It's all on the servers. I'm putting a package together.'

'No! Abu Salem has been caught. We have to get the reactions from the Mumbai underworld. I'm calling Mumbai.'

Within minutes several people returned to the office, which had been emptying out. A wave of excitement ran from the newsroom to the production control room. Homi's heart began to thud when Salem was seen climbing the stairs into an aircraft, handcuffed to Indian policemen. When the doors were shut, her thudding heart turned into a shiver than ran straight down her spine. Which was when a voice behind her asked, 'Are you all right?'

Homi spun around to find a slim, fair stranger, as tall as her, standing with a sheaf of documents in his hand. His face was angular, with close-cropped, thick black hair. Dressed in jeans and a handloom kurta, he exuded the air of a globe-trotting, adventure-loving photographer.

'You seem thrilled,' he said, a superior look on his face. 'Are you obsessed with the underworld?'

Homi didn't know what to say.

'Why do you look like that? Are you frightened?'

'Abu Salem has been caught,' she said. 'Now, I hope Dawood, Chhota Shakeel, Anees, all those criminals are also caught, quickly.'

'Have I seen you before?' he asked straight out.

'I've no idea.'

'Are you new here? No, of course you're not.'

'How can you tell?'

'Newcomers don't have such confidence.'

Confidence? But Homi had lost that a long time ago.

'But you're new,' she said, 'I haven't seen you before, yet you don't look to lack confidence your-self.'

'I joined just before Durga Puja.'

'First time on night shift?'

'Yes, I was on the day shift so I'd just left, but Yash called me back.'

'I see. So you've proved yourself capable of challenging assignments.'

'I never see you on the day shift.'

'I'm only here nights.'

'Yash told me we need a good producer to take charge of the night shift.'

'In that case we'll see each other every day.'

'Let's see if it suits me first. I never stayed up late or woke up early to study.'

'What did you study?'

'Media Studies. J.U. My name's Chetan Chowdhury.'

'Chetan? Are you Bengali?'

'It's Chaitanya, actually.'

'I'm Homi, I'm in charge of lifestyle – I mean, I was.'

Just then, her mobile rang.

'Tell me, Yash.'

'Hi, Homi. You sound excited.'

'Yes, I am.'

'You sound like your old self. Seems you've managed to shake off your depression at last.'

Chetan walked off towards his desk.

'There's lots on, Homi. Winter's coming, so why don't you do an autumn–winter story – food, clothes, holidays, parties. And weren't you thinking of a story on midlife crisis? Go home tonight, take tomorrow off, come back on your regular shift from the day after.'

Chetan had put a pair of headphones on. He was probably listening to music, for his lips were moving while his fingers flew over his keyboard. Suddenly he said loudly,

'Six stories in the 8 AM package today, all right?'

Taking the phone out into the corridor, Homi sat down on a chair and lit a cigarette.

'Give me a few days more, Yash,' she said.

Yash was silent for a few moments.

'All right, take your time.'

—

'Both of you are lucky that way – your mother doesn't turn to you for help. But what really surprises me, Khuku, is that you chose to get a job, to earn a living. Just look at Oli. You could have had a life like hers. Instead, you fell head over heels in love with an ordinary boy, and went and got married. And now that job has squeezed the life out of you.

'You could have led a life of luxury, Khuku, if you'd married into Gora Sengupta's family. They were so fond of you. Just the other day, Aloka came up to me at Krishna Modi's house, said, *"If only you'd given me your daughter, Mrs Banerjee."* But you've stopped taking care of yourself, Khuku, no one's going to give you a second look now. If you could at least have kept your marriage going ...'

Mrs Banerjee retrieved a box of sweets from the fridge and offered Homi one.

'Mita came over, she kept wailing that she wasn't able to do anything for me. So I told her, why don't you take me to the hills for a holiday? Only, what will happen to your father if I go on a holiday, Khuku? Will you stay here and look after him?'

Homi didn't even look at the sweet. She might have tried it if it had still been fresh.

Her father had had a catheter put in, and it seemed there was an infection. Dr Ghosh was due to come and see him, but he wouldn't be there before 9:30. It was him Homi was waiting for at Belvedere Road. Once he turned up, she would go straight to the office for her night shift.

Instead of answering her mother, Homi threw out a question of her own.

'Did you ever have a good relationship with Mr

Banerjee, Ma? Even briefly?'

'What are you talking about?'

'You did give birth to Oli, after all,' Homi said quietly. 'That's proof you had some conjugal life.'

Her mother bristled.

'That was a one-time thing, Khuku, one single time. Do you understand?'

She stomped off to the kitchen, but soon returned.

'Mr Banerjee, he … he wasn't up to it. Should I tell you more? You want to hear more? How old was I, no more than twenty-one or twenty-two. You think I didn't feel desire? I used to quarrel with him every day, and run off to my parents. And it wasn't just … that, that he couldn't give me. I never got any love or affection from him, either. And then the impudence of his mother and her daughters! Aristocrats in name, but very small-minded people.'

Dr Ghosh lived in Jodhpur Park. After examining Homi's father he gave her a lift to Southern Avenue, from where she took a taxi to her office, arriving at 10:30. As always, Homi went straight to the cafeteria, carrying her tray to the table where Gouri was eating by herself. Rotis, chicken stew, salad and a sweet, with a paneer curry for vegetarians – that was the menu tonight.

'So, you're on night shift?' Homi asked Gouri.

Gouri looked up at her.

'I still have some work to finish. I'm going to do it, no matter how long it takes. So for now, dinner.'

'You seem really into your food.'

'I'm starving.'

'So am I.'

Gouri observed her carefully.

'You look fresh, Homi, just like you used to. Is everything all right again?'

Gouri sounded stressed.

'What's wrong?' Homi asked.

'Priyanshu and I broke up six months ago.'

'I heard.'

Gouri and Priyanshu had fallen in love as students, both at the film institute in Pune. After returning to Kolkata they had begun to live together, in a flat in Lake Gardens, which was when they had discovered that they weren't really compatible.

'Priyanshu wrote me a letter last week. He wanted to meet up with me. So we met. And he made me a proposal.'

'What kind of proposal?'

'He wants to marry me.'

'Really?' Homi smiled. 'So he's coming back to you?'

Gouri shook her head. 'Not exactly. He's been

offered the chance to work with a major film production company in France. But getting a visa is very
difficult these days. It's easier if you're married, and
your wife has a job in India. So.'

Gouri's eyes were brimming with tears. Homi
had dipped a piece of her roti in the stew but now
couldn't raise it to her mouth.

'Such a humiliating proposition,' Gouri said. 'And
still I couldn't say no to him, Homi. He left me, he
never cared for me, he ran a steam-roller over my
heart — and yet, all I thought was, how can I let him
lose out on such a great opportunity? He got it on
merit, after all. *"Our relationship has no future,"* he told
me, *"but help me out all the same."'*

'Isn't there anyone else he could ask?' Homi said.
'Why does it have to be you?'

'Because he knows I will give him a divorce
whenever he wants. Apparently, he has enormous
confidence in me. I mustn't think of the marriage as a
chain, he told me, I can do whatever I want, he won't
make any objections.'

'Priyanshu will make excellent films,' Homi said.
'That's for sure.'

'So we put in the notice for a registered marriage
today. Then he flew off to Mumbai. The thing is,
first he said we'd live together for a little while and

then get married, then he said he can't live with me, now he's making all these demands of me, confident that I'll go along with whatever, but even through all of this, my love for him hasn't changed. I quite liked signing that form. I did want to marry him.'

As Gouri left, Chetan entered, and sat down at Homi's table. He was looking handsome, in khakis with a handloom shirt, and carefully cultivated stubble on his cheeks. The two of them had been working together every day. He'd worn a bulky black jacket all through the winter, but now, in the middle of February, the chill had finally vanished. Without the jacket Chetan looked different, streamlined.

'How's the chicken?' he asked.

'Pretty good. Too oily, though.'

'I'll have it anyway. It's my last day here. I was looking for you.'

Homi was jolted by this unexpected statement. Last day? It was largely because of Chetan that the night shift had grown increasingly attractive to her.

'Sounds like all of you have great fun on the night shift, Homi,' some day shift colleagues had started to comment.

Aditya, Souvik and a few others would stay behind for a taste of the fun. It was true, there were celebrations, arguments, quarrels, singing. Chetan had caused a sensation one night by pinning a poster of Janis Joplin's famous nude on the wall. Take it down, some demanded. Keep it, others said. Yash took the poster away the following morning, saying he was going to put it up in his bedroom.

There was another thing about Chetan that Homi marvelled at. He was carefree when chatting with friends, but changed completely when in work mode, hurling print-outs across the hall if the copy didn't satisfy him. If he found mistakes in the work done during the day he would wake the culprit up in the middle of the night to shout at them down the phone. He had more or less become Yash's night-time counterpart. Sometimes, if Yash needed him in the morning, he'd stay on despite having spent all night in the office.

'Last day,' Homi echoed.

'Why?'

'I have to transfer to the head office.'

'You put in for it?'

'No, the company just decided to move me.'

'You must be very pleased.'

'Why?'

'Moving to Mumbai means working at the national level. Greater challenges, a bigger salary.'

'Yeah, I'm aware of that. But there's a lot here I

really like. I'll miss that if I go.'

'When are you leaving?'

'Sunday morning.'

'So this will be your last day at the office.'

'No, I'll keep coming in. I like it. You're here.'

Homi had finished eating, and got up to rinse her hands when Chetan spoke her name. She turned back to face him. His eyes sent her an unusual signal, but one that she was familiar with. She had seen eyes like these before, the look in them unmistakable. She had seen Chetan in various moods over the past three months, but never with eyes like these, never with a voice like this.

Chetan grabbed her hand, which had remnants of food on the fingers.

'I have something to tell you, Homi.'

Everyone else in the cafeteria was watching them.

'Let me wash my hands first,' she said.

'Can we go out for a bit?'

He spoke loudly enough for everyone to hear.

It was past eleven. They went out for a stroll along AJC Bose Road.

Chetan broke the silence when they were near Minto Park, about a kilometre from the office.

'I'm about to utter some clichés,' he said, stopping in front of Hindustan International. 'Let's go in.

Nothing but five-star hotels open at this hour.'

He put his hand lightly on her back.

The first-floor lounge was empty, so they had their pick of the sofas.

'Listen, Homi, I don't have much time. I want to know what you think of me. Are you going to deny that you like me? I told Yash about my feelings for you. *"Control yourself,"* he told me, *"Homi isn't well, she can't handle emotional stress right now. Just try to be her friend. Make her smile."* You tell me, Homi, haven't I tried to make you smile?'

Down a short corridor in this same hotel was the banquet hall where Homi had first met Lalit, on a rather similar night.

'Are you still married, Homi?' Chetan asked.

Lalit. Was she still Lalit's wife or not?

'Everyone says you broke down because your marriage didn't work out. Is that the truth? Are you depressed because of your break-up?'

As he spoke, Homi felt her body, her heart, her limbs turn to stone. And her brain? Frozen.

'I noticed you the very first day. I liked you as soon as I saw you. And now I'm in love with you. I'll never hurt you, you can trust me.'

Homi sighed. Chetan winked at her.

'Listen, I'm not letting you go, not unless you tell

me, *no, I don't like you at all.* And you'll never be able to say it, because I'll shut you up with the hardest kiss ever.'

The smile had completely left his face. A nerve had become visible on his temple, his eyebrows were contorted, and he was staring at her lips.

'A little while ago, when there was a spot of stew on your lips, I was dying to lick it up. Oof, Homi, can I kiss you?'

He brushed his left thumb across her lips.

Homi's body caught fire at his touch. She had been turned to stone, but it took no time for the stone to melt. Sitting on the soft sofa with her hands in her lap like a helpless little girl, she felt her panty flooding at just this touch, at a mere proposition, at the most fleeting contact. And she felt the desire to start a new partnership, to dive into a new act of lovemaking, to let herself be carried away on an endless current of love, lust and craving.

In a trance, she said, 'Kiss me.'

Chetan hesitated.

'First tell me if you love me.'

'Can't we kiss unless I love you?'

'I've kissed many women that way,' Chetan admitted as he touched her cheek. 'But I don't want a loveless kiss from someone I love.'

'Lalit wanted the same thing,' Homi told him. 'He wanted love, because he was in love. But being in love isn't a sufficient foundation to build a relationship. A relationship develops only when someone wants love in exchange for love. And then fate is imposed on them.'

'Fate? Why fate?'

'Fate is everything. Don't you see it?'

Chetan gazed at her with expressionless eyes.

'Don't tell anyone, Chetan,' she said, 'but my fate stalks me constantly. It doesn't want me to enter into a relationship. It wants me all to itself. I ought to belong to it alone. I know I sound like a raving lunatic, but it's true.'

'How long has this been going on? Since when has fate been stalking you?'

'A long time now.'

'I'll tell you something, Homi, no one should be on the night shift continuously. You'd better stop. Take a break, go on holiday, then start working regular hours. Everything will turn out fine, you'll see.'

'Maybe.' But she didn't sound convinced.

'I feel terrible, Homi. If I weren't going away, I'd have made you forget all these strange ideas of yours. We'd have worked hard, partied hard, gone on holidays together. You'd have laughed again, without a care in the world.'

'But I have no desire to laugh, Chetan. Or to cry, either. Laughter and tears seem equally stupid to me – imposed, artificial, predestined.'

'Who told you all this?'

'Mr Vaid. A palmist.'

'Where's he from?'

'Kolkata.'

'Does he have an office somewhere?'

'Yes, at Jagu Bazaar.'

'What are his hours?'

'Seven to ten every evening.'

'Right, I'll go and see him tomorrow, see what sort of bullshit he feeds me. What's his address?'

'I don't know the address. I just happened across the place. But by then I was already being stalked by a hermit.'

'Very well, let me at least get one thing done before I leave – let me break the nose of this so-called palmist. Come with me, show me where to find him.'

'Now?'

'Yes, now. And then I'll take you home.'''

Chetan manoeuvred her into a taxi, asking, 'Where's your fate? Anywhere nearby?'

Homi gripped his arm, and he turned to look at her. 'Don't be afraid. I'm here.'

She nodded. At Jagu Bazaar, they began to walk along the pavement. Crates were being unloaded from large lorries, the porters looking half-asleep as they went about their work in utter silence. Homi wound her way through them to the spot where she had seen the signboard, only to find that it wasn't there. She looked in every direction, but could see neither the signboard nor the narrow entrance through which she had walked in.

'Where is it?' Chetan asked. 'Are you sure we're in the right place?'

'Yes, it was here,' she said, but doubtfully. 'An old red building.'

'You must have imagined it. There's nothing here, no Mr Vaid the palmist. Come on, I'll take you home.'

'It's not a home, it's a boarding house,' Homi corrected him.

'Well, let me take you there, then.'

Chetan looked very worried. Homi felt he was hers, more than Lalit had ever been.

He dropped her off outside her boarding house and said, 'Believe me, Homi, there's no such thing as fate or fate. Only birth and death are inevitable — everything else is in your hands. Circumstances play a huge role in our lives, but we ourselves can make or break those circumstances. What you're forgetting is that we're human beings, we have no choice but to believe in the power of work. Read Vivekananda, Homi, read Aurobindo, you'll see how they've written against the idea of predestination. Fate is nothing, fate is no one, we alone have an influence over what happens, so ignore fate, don't surrender to it. And even if you consider fate an unshakeable truth, don't keep standing on the edge of this flowing river called life – dive into the water, swim in it for all you're worth. There's no such thing as the future, time is like a wheel that keeps rolling, so our present is also our future. Come on, Homi, life may be Sisyphus pushing the rock uphill, but still, you must apply yourself to it.'

When she rang the bell by the large wooden door of her boarding house, one of the fairies of the night came to open the door before vanishing back inside. Chetan held out his arms and, forgetting all compulsions, forgetting all her fear and hesitation, forgetting a fate she could not explain, Homi threw herself into them, rubbing her face on his chest.

'Take me away, far away.'

'Will you come to Mumbai? Tell me. I'm ready, Homi.'

She wept and wept. She couldn't remember the last time she had cried.

'I'll go wherever you take me,' she told him, and

he touched her lips with his. Not a kiss: it was as though he was trying to understand her lips with his. As soon as they touched Homi slipped into a trance, like a possessed being who had spent an entire age without sleep. But a stab of unease made her open her eyes, only to discover it was not Chetan but the man with the matted locks embracing her, his lips like black scorpions, his eyes flashing lightning, his hair, beard and moustache giving off the smell of a forest that had lain in darkness for centuries. Those were not arms but the coils of a serpent around her. She screamed, trying to free herself, but failing.

'What's the matter, Homi?' Chetan asked.

Now she saw it was Chetan. Yes, Chetan. Could fate itself convey instructions to ignore fate? Could fate itself provide the resolution to the problem it had created? Ha ha! What a cruel joke. She shoved Chetan away.

'Homi, Homi, come with me,' he begged.

She saw a taxi emerging from a road on her right. Leaping into it, Homi shrieked, 'Take me away, far away!'

## BENARAS – A SECOND RETURN TO HER SENSES

When Homi opened her eyes, her gaze settled on a face with a large vermilion dot on the forehead. There was another smudged yellow dot next to it, above eyes lined thickly with kohl. The woman gazed at Homi from different angles. She was about the same age, dark-skinned, dressed in a maroon sari and a matching sleeveless blouse. Her garments were wet, clinging to her. A mass of loose hair hung down her back, and her arms were adorned with glass bangles of different colours. She wasn't particularly beautiful, but her voluptuous body was taut and electric.

She was obviously a Bengali.

'So, how do you feel?' she asked Homi in Bangla, then left the room without waiting for a reply.

Homi sat up slowly and looked carefully around her. She was in a strange room, almost completely dark. The small wooden door opposite her was open, so she could see a large, open terrace, bathed in sunlight. A rustic cot lay outside, with some sort of poppadoms set to dry on its woven rope surface. Next to it stood several jars of pickles.

From the intensity of the sunlight Homi concluded that it couldn't be more than 11 AM. How bright it was outside, yet so dark in here. There were no windows in the high-ceilinged room, only several openings just below the roof, each about a foot wide, covered by what appeared on close inspection to be stone latticework. The same rough stone, a mixture of saffron and brown, had been used for the floor of the room and of the terrace outside. Homi had never seen a room like this before, certainly not of these dimensions. It seemed to belong to a mansion. The rafters high above her head had layers of tar on them. It was clearly a very old building, but well-maintained.

There was a chorus of voices outside, all of them female, accompanied by the clink of bangles. Someone could be heard singing a devotional song, the sound coming not from the terrace but through the wall behind Homi. Homi tried to focus. Where had she ended up? Considering the other woman's solicitous question, and how she had left the door wide open, it didn't seem to be anywhere sinister.

Then she caught sight of a gigantic lizard on the

wall in front of her, and froze. It was huge! Its tail was curved under its own weight. As Homi experienced a strange dread, someone appeared at the door. But she didn't dare look away from the lizard to find out who it was. Out of the corner of her eye, she could see a small crowd behind the person, silent and orderly. Only their bangles were audible.

She realised, even with her eyes glued to the lizard, that a woman was approaching her.

'Are you afraid of this creature?' the newcomer asked in English.

Her eyes smarting, Homi nodded.

'Get rid of it,' the woman instructed someone in Hindi.

A murmur rose from the small group outside, with one, perhaps two of them laughing. Then someone came forward with a long stick. Homi stared at the lizard, her jaws clamped together, till it slithered out through the latticed opening. The reptile dragged its bloated belly, seeming to move with difficulty. Homi's own body felt like it would collapse with fatigue.

'It's gone.'

Finally Homi looked at the woman, and saw that she was startlingly beautiful. She had never seen such a lovely woman in Kolkata. Five foot eight or nine, amply built, with broad shoulders and thighs like pillars, though without an ounce of fat. Her heavy breasts were bursting through her cream muslin sari, and even the rounded moon of her navel was exceedingly deep. A large diamond stud adorned her delicate nose, with smaller diamonds flashing from her ears. On her right wrist sat a watch with a narrow black strap, and the gold bangles on her left arm were interspersed with diamond ones. Her throat was bare, but her voice was so sparklingly clear and gorgeous that it could be called an ornament in its own right. The intelligence in her small, almond-shaped eyes overpowered the grace in them. She radiated such nobility that Homi gazed at her spellbound, realizing as she did that this was the owner of the mansion, the one who controlled everyone present, accustomed to wielding a liberal form of power.

Homi opened her mouth to speak, but she was interrupted by the Bengali woman in the maroon sari, who said tauntingly,

'Want a mosquito-net? Benaras is full of lizards, you can't afford to be afraid of them. There are even larger reptiles here.'

'Don't tease her, Chandra,' the regal woman objected mildly.

Then she turned to Homi.

'Would you like some tea?'

'How did I get here?' Homi asked in Bangla.

'When? What day is it? Ah, I mean, how …'

'I understand Bangla,' the woman reassured her. 'My guru's was a man called Yagneshwar Bhattacharya. He didn't speak a word of Hindi.'

She touched her earlobe in a traditional gesture of respect before sitting down on the bed.

'Chandra brought you here yesterday. You went up to her at Dashashwamedh Ghat and took her hand, you were very frightened by something.'

Homi asked again what the date was.

'The twenty-second of February,' the woman said. So three days had passed. Homi remembered checking the time on her mobile while searching for Mr Vaid's chamber with Chetan − 12:45 AM, February 19th. What had happened in between? She could remember barely anything, only a fragmented scene or two. Had she lost her memory? How strange!

'Where's my bag and my mobile?'

This was the first thing that occurred to her.

The women in the room exchanged glances.

'You had nothing with you,' Chandra said.

'We won't bother you with questions now. Have some tea, rest a bit if you like, Aina here will stay with you, she'll help you with everything. Bring the lady a toothbrush, please.'

'You think I'm going to bother her, Bibirani?' asked Chandra.

'You can stay with her if you promise not to disturb her,' said the woman, lifting an admonishing finger.

But Chandra stayed silent.

She turned back to Homi.

'What should we call you?'

Not only was her voice pleasing, Homi thought, her manner of speaking was elegant too, revealing the respect in which she held people. She was clearly granting Homi great importance already. But Bibirani? Was that her name?

'My name is Homi.'

'You're absolutely safe here. No one can do you any harm. Rest now. Ask Chandra if you need anything, she's already in love with you.'

Bibirani was halfway out the door when she turned back to Homi.

'Does anyone have to be informed? Do you want to make a call?'

Homi thought it over, then shook her head.

'In that case, we will meet again after lunch.'

Homi still didn't know who the woman was, but the atmosphere and people here were so new to her, so unusual, that everything began to leave a mark. She found herself warming to the woman addressed as Bibirani, who was followed by two others when she left, leaving Chandra and two others in the room. One of them, around twenty years old, said,

'You've lost your phone, your bag, everything?'

Homi had had money in her bag, her credit and debit cards, her press card, and countless other important things. She knew the Belvedere Road and office phone numbers, but all her other contacts were only saved on her mobile phone. Losing them meant losing the story of her life. An elderly man dressed in a dhoti and shirt entered with a cup of tea on a tray. Was the tray made of silver? The cup and saucer were milk-white.

'Please drink it while it's hot,' he said, smiling deferentially. 'You'll enjoy it.'

Homi couldn't remember where she had spent the past three days. She couldn't have bathed, didn't remember whether she had eaten or even brushed her teeth. A small group of strangers was staring at her now. All of them had curiosity written on their faces, but they were so cooperative that the question, 'Who are these people?' was not foremost in Homi's mind. Right then, in fact, she was surprisingly relaxed. With her bag and phone missing, she was feeling more isolated than usual, and didn't want to spend a single moment thinking about her situation. Much better to immerse herself in the truth that, for now, she was here, in this building, amongst these people. Had she done anything to upset the equations of existence? No, she was still whirling within the circle of fate.

Chandra sat down on Homi's bed.

'You've been sleeping since last evening – do you want to go on sleeping or would you rather get up?'

'I want to have a wash.'

'Shall I help you?'

'No.'

'I'll bring you another cup of tea when you're done,' the elderly man said in Hindi.

Homi followed Chandra out of the room. Outside, she paused. The terrace was enormous, with rooms on all sides. Those on her left and right had windows with no shutters. A staircase with the same stone latticework at its sides led to the roof. It, too, was made of stone, the floor was noticeably uneven. All the floors were uneven, a special feature of this mansion.

The space Chandra thrust her into, claiming it was the bathroom, was in fact a labyrinth, and had no door. They took several sharp turns along a narrow passage before arriving at a small terrace, which was almost dark. It was difficult to identify the source of the dim light. There was a tank brimming with water, but on closer observation Homi realised that this

ancient bathroom actually had several modern facili-
ties, including a shower. Chandra left Homi waiting
there, and her skin was beginning to prickle when the
woman returned with a new toothbrush and a tube
of toothpaste.

'Isn't there a light in here?' Homi asked.

'Oh, I forgot, let me switch it on.' Chandra disappeared again. The light came on a little later, but
the darkness and the cold rising from the stone floor
couldn't care less. Chandra returned.

'You gripped my arm so hard yesterday you can still
see the mark. Someone must have fed you something
bad. There you were, wandering around Benaras, out
of your senses, it's honestly a wonder you didn't fall
into some creep's clutches. The gods here must have
been especially kind to you. What did you say your
name is, again? Hema?'

Benaras! Of course. Bibirani had mentioned
Dashashwamedh Ghat. It was a familiar name, but
things weren't adding up for Homi. How did she get
to Benaras, so far away from Kolkata, with no memory of the journey in between? It was a question she
would rather not ponder.

'Can you recall why you came here? You couldn't
explain anything last night. Bibirani will corner you
as soon as you get a little stronger. Why are you here,

who did you come with, where do you live – she'll want to know everything. The senior police officers here are all under her thumb. Even if you don't want to reveal anything, it'll only take her a minute to find out.'

Homi's palms were grimy, and her feet were dirty too. She asked Chandra for soap. 'Use as much water as you need to,' Chandra said, 'but these clothes won't do. I'll bring you a towel. My sari and blouse would fit you, but Bibirani says you're not just someone who's wandered in off the streets, so I can't give you my clothes. Let me see what I can do.'

Homi sat down on the broad edge of the tank to wait for Chandra.

'I never would have imagined this,' she said on her return. She sounded genuinely surprised by something.

'Imagined what?'

Homi's heart trembled. She didn't want to have to return to Kolkata, not under any circumstances.

'Bibirani told me to give you Barkha's clothes. All this time, we weren't even allowed to touch them.'

Homi stared at Chandra as the latter handed her a sparkling white cotton salwar-kameez.

'These belonged to Bibirani's daughter.'

'Where is she?'

'She went to Mumbai to study. She doesn't keep in touch with her mother anymore.'

'Why not?'

'Because … she belongs to a different section of society now. She's got an education, her friends are from well-known families, they'll drop her if they find out who her mother is. You know that company Reliance? That's where Barkha works now. Earns a hundred and fifty thousand a month. What does she need her mother for? Her boyfriend is from a rich family. Bibirani understands, she never asks her daughter to visit her. But of course she's sad about it. I know, because she loves me very much. She takes me with her wherever she goes. We've been around India five times in the ten years I've been with her. But now she's stopped going out, not even in Benaras, unless it's one of the handful of families she can't say no to. When the Singhs of Ramgarh had their first grandchild the eldest daughter-in-law pleaded with Bibirani to sing. But what will happen when she stops altogether, Hema? I doubt if you'll find more than three or four courtesans in Benaras who can truly sing and dance. If you could have seen how the women fawned over her! They passed their babies to her, they said, "*You bring them up, Bibirani. Who else can teach them how to be sophisticated and cultured? Only a blue-*

*blooded courtesan can do it."* But that didn't mean Barkha wanted to follow in her mother's footsteps. That era is over. It will end completely the day Bibirani is cremated at Manikarnika Ghat.'

'Is she a Hindu?'

'Yes. Manekabai. That's her name.'

Homi brushed her teeth.

'None of the girls here bathe on their own, they have to be given a bath and then a massage. Shall I do that for you now?'

'What time is it, do you think?' Homi asked.

'Around twelve.'

Twelve noon. The hour at which Homi was usually asleep on her narrow bed in an empty boarding house. In the office at this moment, journalists, editors, producers, anchors, camerapeople, tech support, adding up to over a hundred people, would all be shouting at the same time. As for her, did she have any control over the fact that right now she was standing in this bathroom with a stone floor?

'But I'm not one of the girls here,' she told Chandra.

'No harm in enjoying the privileges.'

'All right, then.'

'Get naked,' Chandra said.

Unembarrassed, Homi took off her jeans, shirt, bra and panty. Chandra poured water on the discarded clothes, then unbound Homi's hair.

'Your sari was wet when I saw you this morning,' Homi said. 'Were you giving someone else a bath?'

'Yes, I was helping Bari Ma. Bibirani's grand-mother. She's ninety, but still so pretty.'

'I wouldn't have thought she could have a grand-mother still alive.'

'Of course. Bibirani's mother, grandmother, great-aunt, all of them live here. Only her sister Jahnavibai lives next door, alone. She has a tumour in her brain. She won't live much longer, and she's suffered a lot already.'

Chandra soaped Homi all over, rubbed her feet with a pumice stone, and poured water over her.

'Aina will wash your clothes and put them out to dry,' she said as she gently towelled Homi's hair. After putting on Barkha's clothes, Homi made her way back through the labyrinth to the mirror in the dressing-room, where her reflection made her think she was someone else. It wasn't just her life's trajec-tory, she felt, but life itself that had changed.

'I don't know who you are,' said Chandra, 'but I feel I've known you a long time. Why can't you tell me what's wrong with you? You didn't seem in a normal frame of mind when I saw you yesterday, but you don't look that way anymore. Are you feeling better? Once you've recovered, you'll want to get back to wherever it was you were going, I'm sure. But Bibirani won't let you go easily, take my word for it.'

Emerging from the labyrinth, Homi heard a woman singing, accompanied by the notes of a harmonium and the droning of a tanpura, along with a number of male and female voices in the background. These other voices were following the lead of the first singer. Classical music rehearsals were in progress in one of the rooms on the right hand side of the terrace, the melody breathing life into the inert stone mansion. With the day advancing, there was an air of increased activity. Most importantly, seven or eight monkeys of different sizes were sitting on the stairs leading to the roof. In one corner of the terrace, someone was stuffing an old mattress with fresh cotton, a process which the monkeys were observing carefully.

Everything here was new and different. The colours were unfamiliar, the smells too. It was as though Homi was watching a film.

'What are all these monkeys doing here?'

'You're new, so be careful,' Chandra told her. 'They'll try to grab your food when they see you eating.'

She led Homi not to the earlier room but a new

one, with an old-fashioned bed about ten feet long
and ten feet wide, a mirror that stretched across an
entire wall, and tall, wide wooden cupboards. The
elderly man brought her tea again, in a porcelain
cup on a silver tray, along with savouries and sweets.
Homi sipped the tea, to which thickened milk had
been added. It all gave her a deep sense of well-be-
ing. The potato curry served with the flaky kachauri
smelled and tasted so enticing that she forgot where
she was and cleaned the plate.

'You must have been famished,' Chandra commented with a smile.

'These are delicious,' Homi said.

'Naturally. They come from a shop that everyone
in the world visits. Even the foreigners taking music
lessons from Bibirani will all rush there when they
leave.'

Homi's eyes widened.

'Is that why the singing sounds so strange?'

Chandra laughed.

'Could anyone possibly master this art in only six
months? Still they come in their hundreds to throng
around Bibirani. There's an American boy who could
put all of Benaras to shame. He wakes up at the crack
of dawn, Hema, to bathe in the Ganga and say prayers
for his father. Then he spends the entire day here

practising, refusing to leave before evening. Daniel, he's called.'

'My name isn't Hema.'

'What is it, then?'

'Homi, it's Homi.'

Recalling how Chetan had called her name while she was jumping into a taxi, she felt miserable again. His face had told her that he had just had the surprise of his life.

Were they still talking about her in Kolkata, or was it business as usual already? Would she ever see Chetan again? As Homi pondered these questions, a woman entered the room. She wasn't exactly as dignified as Bibirani, but she obviously didn't belong to the ranks of Chandra or Aina. Scanning Homi from head to toe, she announced, 'It's true, she does look like Barkha,' then left as abruptly as she'd arrived.

'You know who that was?' Chandra said.

'That was Barkha's governess. She brought the girl up single-handed. There must be a real resemblance.'

# GRATITUDE

Chandra just couldn't stop talking. She had so much to say that she didn't even have time to get into a dry sari. Sitting there in Barkha's room, she began recounting Bibirani's history in detail, and Homi got to know everything in the course of the afternoon. This room had an actual window, quite new in comparison to the rest of the building, having been carved out of the wall after the latticework was demolished no more than fifty years earlier. The narrow lane it looked out onto was called Gangabai Ki Galli. There had used to be several other renowned courtesans in this neighbourhood, for one of whom the lane had been named. It filled with water from the Ganga at the height of the rainy season. The lane led to the one with the famous kachauri shop, which in turn went directly to Manikarnika Ghat. Homi realised that the devotional songs she had heard in the morning were being sung somewhere in this lane.

Chandra continued with her stories. More than three hundred years ago, the king of Boondi had visited Benaras with his wife on a pilgrimage. He was accompanied by his courtiers, staff and bodyguards. Maneklal was a member of this entourage, and had brought his young wife along on her request. A month or so passed pleasantly, in rituals, bathing in the holy river, charity for the poor, and listening to devotional songs. But, a day before he was due to leave Benaras, the king of Boondi was attacked by an assassin. The attacker was caught and, before being beheaded, confessed that Maneklal was part of the conspiracy. The king's followers killed Maneklal, but his young wife Kamleshwari managed to escape with the help of her maid. Pregnant and helpless, she sought shelter with a Muslim courtesan near Manikarnika. Eventually, Kamleshwari had a daughter – Hindu society had severed ties with her by then. Her daughter Rajeshwari was the first courtesan in this lineage, which was part of a matrilineal society, so that a girl was known by her mother's identity.

Of course, nobody was ready to swear that Rajeshwaribai's lineage had run unbroken over three hundred years. But the art had always found an inheritor. Sometimes, a courtesan had formally adopted a girl child. Two hundred years ago, a minister from the kingdom of Mathura had given this mansion as a gift to Padminibai, a foremother of Bibirani's.

'What about sons?' Homi asked. 'Didn't any of them give birth to boys?'

'Sons were killed at birth,' said Chandra. 'Or one of the midwives would abandon them on the bank of the Ganga.'

Noticing that Homi had fallen silent, Chandra hastily took it back.

'I made that up.'

'Really?'

'Not everything, but some of it.'

'But you do know a lot of history.'

'If it's history you're after, you must ask Bari Ma. She knows thousands of stories about all the kings. Just take her out on the river, she can tell you every single detail about every house on the bank. Even at this age her memory is incredible. A team from the Discovery Channel made a film about Benaras a year ago, and they stayed here with us for a month. One of them was a professor who spent all day asking Bari Ma questions about the city. This mansion itself is pure history, Homi.'

Suddenly, there was an uproar outside. Two monkeys were running along the terrace, and two of the women were chasing them with sticks.

'What did they take?' Chandra called.

'Biscuits,' someone called back.

'What about your own history, Chandra?' Homi asked.

'We used to live in Bangalitola,' Chandra began without any hesitation or preamble. 'My father was a bookbinder. When he died we virtually became orphans, we were on the brink of starvation. Then my elder sister, five years older, got married, and deposited me with Bibirani's sister Jahnavibai. I've been here ever since.'

'Just like that? What made her choose Jahnavibai?'

'When I was a child, I had seen Jahnavibai bathing at Lalitaghat. I was under her spell from that moment, I longed to see her, I'd look for her everywhere, but no one could tell me where to find her. The top courtesans of Benaras had already begun going into hiding to protect their reputations. There were all these people in the lanes of Dalmandi or Sarnath claiming to be courtesans, but they were just full of talk, they couldn't even tell one raga from another. And the blue-blooded ones like Bibirani had become music teachers in aristocratic families. A thousand rupees a class, but then her kind is beyond the reach of ordinary people, even if they come into money. You can lay five hundred thousand rupees at Bibirani's feet, she'll say, forgive me, just allow me to teach these children their music. I can't put on all these airs. It's true that Bibirani does still perform for handpicked clients, but those are extremely private affairs, not a soul gets to know what she sings, what sari she wears, what jewellery she puts on. She even takes her own water and paan, so that she doesn't have to accept anything from the host. And she leaves as soon as the performance ends. I told you, didn't I, that all the senior police officers here know Bibirani, but not one of them dares ask for a song. She's had to fight to earn this level of respect. It's only Barkha who refused to respect her at all, either as a mother or an artist.

'But my god, if you could have heard Barkha sing. Her notes would make your hair stand on end, your throat would turn dry with admiration. What style, what skill! Her entire body sang. Blood is thicker than water – it's herself she's trying to escape from.'

Homi felt that she knew how difficult this was – to run away from one's own self.

'It was my own doing, making sure I was left with Jahnavibai,' Chandra went on, resting her cheek in a cupped palm.

'Not that Bibirani will ever pour a drop of music into my hands. Her face is like a wall when she's teaching. You could call me mad. Women usually want a home, a lover, children – but this was what I wanted. As for why, I couldn't say.'

'What was it you wanted?'

Homi didn't understand.

'Some people have to watch time closely, Homi, they have to understand how it behaves.'

It was easy to discern why Bibirani loved Chandra so much. She was intelligent, and her body was like fire.

'Don't men bother you?'

Chandra laughed, rocking from side to side.

'One of them does, very much.'

Barkha's governess came back into the room with a glass on a tray. Touching Homi's chin affectionately with her fingertips, she removed the silk doily that had been draped over the glass. Milk. No, it was lassi. Chilled, smothered in cream.

'Drink up,' she said.

Between the savouries, sweets, and now the lassi, Homi had an attack of heartburn.

Late in the afternoon, Bibirani arrived on regal footsteps at the door to Barkha's room, looking tired but indescribably lovely. Homi feared the cataclysmic reactions this woman might evoke, with a smile, a delicate look, or an undulation of her body.

'May I come in?'

'Of course,' Homi stammered, jumping up from the bed. 'Please don't ask me for permission.'

'Shall we go for lunch?' she suggested – Manekabai, or Bibirani.

Lunch was served on large plates resting on low, marble-topped stools, behind which the diners sat on silk mats. It began with puris, followed by ghee-smeared chapatis, then rice accompanied by five varieties of dal and vegetables. There was also a profusion of poppadoms, pickles and curds. It was all vegetarian, and cooked without onion or garlic. Bibirani used her left hand to eat, moving with the same graceful rhythm as though she were performing a classical dance. After the meal, she escorted Homi back to Barkha's room and sat down with her on the bed.

'I don't actually have any questions,' she said in English, 'but if you'd like to tell me your story ...'

Homi sat there with her head bowed, knowing full well she had nothing to say. The logic that underpinned the story of Kamleshwari escaping the king of Boondi's forces to take shelter with a Muslim courtesan was missing from her life – she had nothing as dramatic to recount. She was an independent woman whom no one had ever prevented from acting according to her own desires. She had built and broken relationships at will. Under normal circumstances, she might have taken a plane or train to Benaras, but it was true, violently true, that she had arrived here under pursuit, unaware of where she was fleeing to.

'Is there anything I can do for you?' Bibirani asked. But Homi only shook her head.

'You've given me shelter for the night, you've helped me in every possible way, even though I'm a complete stranger. I can't ask for anything else.'

Bibirani gazed at her in silence. Then, speaking slowly, she said,

'You don't even need help from the police?'

Taking a pair of steel-rimmed glasses out of a sequin-studded bag, she put them on and looked sharply at Homi, who had lapsed back into silence.

'I ask all those who come here for their passport,' Bibirani explained. 'For many years, I've been using this method to size up foreigners. But I cannot ask you for your identity papers, since it wasn't me you came to. You went up to Chandra, who brought you to me because she trusted you. Besides, you've lost your bag and everything in it, so what would you be able to show me?'

'It's wonderful to lose everything,' Homi said. 'It's freedom.'

'Are you unhappy with who you are?'

Bibirani asked this question as though it were absolutely vital.

'If those of us who have never subscribed to a particular faith, who don't believe in god or fate, who know and have known that our relationship with ourselves develops slowly, through our everyday experiences – if we suddenly discover that none of these experiences happens by choice, that everything is predetermined, that happiness and suffering are all predestined, then what attachment can we have to our own identity, Bibirani? Fate is stalking me. If only I could get a glimpse of myself outside its influence, just a flash, a single free moment ...'

Homi trailed off, groping helplessly for words.

'I understand. If you manage to glimpse yourself as you say, then you will know that you exist.'

'Yes, that's right, I exist. But why am I constantly moving towards non-existence, towards not being?'

'I'll take you to Dinanath Pathak this evening. You can ask him.'

'Who's Dinanath Pathak?'

'People consider him a prophet, a seer, an infallible soothsayer. But he's long given up reading people's palms or any other form of astrology. And he's dying now. Still, if he wishes to say something when he sees you, he will. An audience with him is impossible, of course – for ordinary people, that is. But I have access to his family.'

All the rooms in the mansion turned dark before evening fell. The lanes around the building were dark anyway, with the sunlight kept at bay even in the daytime. The devotional songs had stopped for a while during Homi and Bibirani's conversation – they resumed now. A little later, bells began to ring, followed by the sounds of small prayer gongs. Sitting in the darkness with all these sounds around her, a languid feeling stole over Homi's body. She began to feel so comfortable, she had such a sense of peace, that it was like being born in a world of new sensations.

This time it was Chandra who came in with the tea. Even the clinking of her bangles was soothing.

'Daniel will arrive in a while,' Bibirani said almost inaudibly. 'Tell him to come back tomorrow. I'm taking Homi to Pathak-ji tonight.'

Chandra came closer in the darkness, lowering her lips to Homi's ears.

'Don't leave me,' she whispered.

But Bibirani heard her.

'What is this passion you have for attracting people, Chandra?' she said.

'Will you let me stay with you, Bibirani?' Homi asked.

## WHY WAS SHE HERE?

Bibirani led Homi through a succession of lanes to Dinanath Pathak's house, with Chandra walking on ahead. The sounds of bells and gongs was a constant accompaniment. There was a profusion of temples large and small, even some in the hollows of tree-trunks, and so many narrow, muddy lanes winding up and down inclines that the city felt like a culture of secrecy, a place of clandestine acts. The more piety a person wanted to accumulate, and the more this wish was fulfilled, the more they sought concealment and privacy.

Meanwhile, the narrower the lanes, the larger the cows seemed to be – all of them sacred, of course. They made Homi nervous, and Chandra laughed.

'What are you laughing at?' Bibirani chided her.

A number of policemen were gathered in one spot, sitting on chairs. Chandra and Bibirani stopped to take off their shoes, joined their palms in prayer and bowed their heads, both facing the same direction.

'Over there, that's the back wall of the temple of Baba Vishwanath.'

Here they turned right into a lane. Homi gathered from the conversation between Bibirani and Chandra that Dinanath Pathak's mansion, which was several hundred years old, stood at the end of this lane called Kunja Gali. The lane narrowed as they walked down it, eventually no wider than four or five feet. Groups of ten or so people passed them in succession, each carrying a corpse on a pallet. She realised that the bodies were being taken to Manikarnika, the cremation ground whose pyres had not gone out in thousands of years. Bibirani had covered her head with a fine silk shawl, but still people kept turning round to stare at her. She paid no attention to them, though, seemingly walking in a trance. All three of them were walking, Homi thought, but the journey was this woman's alone.

It was like the sanctum sanctorum of a haunted house – almost entirely dark, without a single window. On a cot in a corner stretched the bony figure of an old man, his body covered with a red blanket. His age was beyond calculation. Bibirani spooned a little water from a bowl to his lips, then told Homi,

'Move the blanket off his feet and touch them with your forehead.'

Homi was frightened at the prospect – she was overcome by dread. Her hands shook uncontrollably, while tears rolled from her eyes. She sweated with an unknown fear.

'Don't disobey me,' Bibirani told her, 'do as I say.'

'I can't, I can't,' Homi babbled.

'Shame on you!' But then the old man spoke.

'It's not her fault, she can't do it.'

'Why is she here, Baba?' Bibirani asked in a softer voice.

'What do you mean, here?'

'Here in Benaras.'

'That's the answer. Arriving at Benaras is the answer.'

'Can't you say anything more, Dinanath-ji?'

He gestured to her.

'He's asking you to write something, Homi,' Bibirani told her. 'One word, just a single word.'

A single word. What was this word that she should write, that had already been determined as the one she would write? What was this word that would prove her identity? Should she turn her life upside down in search of it? All the words in all the languages she knew were flowing past like a stream of vehicle headlights seen from an aircraft window, and Homi was trying to pick just one of them. A single word. But she couldn't get a grip on herself. It was like paper windmills caught in a whirlwind – she was seeking a word with the same breathless desperation. Bibirani pointed to a niche in one of the walls, which held a pen and paper. Homi picked it up and wrote on it, a single, potent word, in large English letters. *Confinement.*

Homi saw herself intimately in this word. She handed the piece of paper to Bibirani, who held it in front of Dinanath Pathak's eyes. Squinting at it, the old man exclaimed, 'Oh lord, oh cruel one!'

# HOMI'S PROMENADE

Because of her bout of heartburn in the afternoon, Homi skipped dinner despite Chandra's insistence. Bibirani hadn't said a word to her on the way back from Dinanath Pathak's house – except to thank her when, slipping on a banana skin, Homi had grabbed her arm to prevent her from falling. Bibirani's expression was sullen, but her natural grace remained. When they returned to the mansion, she disappeared without a word into the room where she practised her music and taught her students. Chandra, who had not entered Dinanath Pathak's room, asked Homi what had happened. Hesitantly, Homi explained that her refusal to touch Dinanath Pathak's feet had provoked Bibirani's anger.

Chandra blanched.

'Oh god, why did you do that? Don't you know who he is? Bibirani will never forgive you!'

'I was frightened.'

'Frightened of what?'

Homi was silent.

'Tell me,' Chandra insisted.

But Homi couldn't answer.

'There really is something wrong with you. Do you know the lengths political leaders go to just to meet him? They camp outside his mansion for days.'

The strains of the tanpura drifted across the terrace.

'I can't tell what Bibirani has in store for you now,' said Chandra. 'Wait here, I'll be back soon.'

She returned soon afterwards.

'Here, take this money, Homi.'

Two hundred rupees, in four fifty-rupee notes. Homi had put on her bra and panty earlier in the evening though they hadn't yet fully dried. Returning her jeans and shirt to her, Chandra told her to put them on quickly.

'Bibirani might ask you to leave at any moment. If she does, I won't be able to help you. These people are snakes by nature, extremely vengeful. You disobeyed her, you insulted Dinanath-ji. There'll be no forgiveness for you now.'

Homi Dutta, or Homi Basu, whatever – she could have been gyrating her hips in a Kolkata nightclub right then. Instead of which, she was standing in Bibirani's stone mansion, penniless, wondering whether the enraged owner was about to throw her out. None of this had happened accidentally. She had pushed herself into this situation. But then, who could say whether that was really true? Although a pure accident was clearly different from something she had willed herself to do, both were acts of fate. That she would spend tonight waiting for Bibirani's decision was itself predetermined.

Fully dressed, Homi sat on Barkha's bed to await Bibirani's instructions. Chandra perched nearby. Gradually, the mansion became silent, the lights going out everywhere except the terrace. Chandra fell asleep, still sitting up. Bibirani had not begun singing yet, and only the droning of the tanpura could be heard. Homi couldn't tell how much time had passed. Eventually, she found Bibirani standing in front of her.

'Why did you refuse to touch his feet?'

'It's not written in the lines on my palm, Bibirani. I cannot show respect to anyone. Reverence, homage, love – all those lines have been wiped out. Or perhaps they were never there. Please believe me.'

Bibirani sighed so deeply that Homi felt her warm breath on her skin.

'How difficult it must be to bear such a life.'

What could Homi possibly say to that?

'Help her into bed, Chandra, and put the mosquito net up.'

Chandra stirred herself and fetched the net from the cupboard.

'Don't forget to change your clothes before you go to bed.'

And with that, Manekabai drifted out of the room.

For a long time, Homi couldn't sleep. She kept imagining that someone was standing by her side.

She had probably fallen asleep around dawn, but Chandra woke her up soon afterwards. She usually went to bathe at Lalitaghat at this hour, before returning home to give Bibirani, her mother and grandmother their baths. Bibirani began her music practice immediately afterwards, with her mother sometimes joining her. Today, Chandra prodded Homi awake.

'Get up, want to come to the ghat with me? You'll love it.'

'No. I won't bathe in the Ganga.'

'Why not? What harm will it do? Bibirani bathes in the river too. Here's a salwar-kameez set. Put it on, wash your face, and come with me. What can be better than a glimpse of Ma Ganga at dawn? I know what a godless creature you are, but whether you believe in god or not, it's a beautiful sight.'

'You bathing in the river, Chandra – now that must be a beautiful sight.'

'It's not about me,' Chandra snapped. 'You're so stubborn, Homi, you're stubborn about everything.'

'How little time it's taken you to get to know me!'

The bells had tolled constantly till late into the night. Homi had been listening at first, but hadn't noticed when they'd stopped. Now the sound had begun churning the air again, along with the words and melodies of devotional songs. She decided to accompany Chandra to the ghat, though she was still determined not to bathe. Getting out of bed, Homi went over to the window that looked out onto the lane, standing there with her fingers wrapped around the bars.

The lane was damp and dirty, hemmed in on both sides by ancient buildings. Directly beneath her was a temple to Hanuman. Homi leaned her head against the bars, watching the scene. And less than half a minute later, there they were – two hermits, deep in conversation as they walked towards the mansion. Her heart leapt into her mouth, but neither of them had matted locks, only saffron turbans wrapped around their heads. One of them spotted her and stopped, and his companion followed suit.

'Give us some tea, my child, serve a saint passing your way.'

Both were getting on in years. The voice was belligerent, the demand, blunt. She recalled being addressed as Empress, that meditative tone, brimming with lust, a macabre personification of her fate. These two were merely well-built human beings, holding small tridents from which hung little ceremonial gun-metal pots.

'We're hungry, child.'

'Forgive us,' said Chandra, 'there's no food to give you so early in the morning.'

They went out, Chandra carrying a jute bag containing her towel and a fresh sari. The smell of ghee was already hanging in the air. Chandra said shop-keepers had started frying the sweets and savouries that people would consume after bathing in the Ganga and offering flowers to the gods.

'Where exactly did I meet you, Chandra?'

'You call that a meeting? You had a mad woman's eyes then, Homi, and you were sobbing fit to burst. I don't know how I managed to get you to the mansion, you're not exactly a small woman. I wasn't even supposed to have been at Dashashwamedh Ghat that evening, but I heard Jayant Misra from Allahabad was here for two days, so I went to listen to him chant hymns to the Ganga. What if I hadn't?'

'You had no choice but to be there, Chandra,' Homi said.

'Let's go to Dashashwamedh, then,' Chandra told her. 'Though it's always crowded, no matter the time.'

Homi had seen this ghat hundreds of times in photographs and films, but this was her first sight of it in real life. Quite some time ago now, she had lost faith in everything but fate. She trusted nothing and no one else. Originally, she had thought her fate was stalking her, but now she wondered whether it wasn't the other way round.

'Benaras is the answer,' Dinanath Batra had said. He was right. Benaras was indeed the answer. She could see that everything was right here – here, every method of surrender was available.

Handing her bag to Homi, Chandra went down into the river. Using her arms to part the water in front of her, she began dipping her head beneath the surface repeatedly. Homi sat down on the wet, silt-covered steps. Several Brahmins with marks of sandalwood paste on their foreheads and tufts of hair sticking from the backs of their heads were seated on mats laid out on cots. They began calling out to her, asking her if she wanted to bathe in the river.

To her left, a circular slab of stone protruded over

the water. It was occupied by a group of hermits, who were already smoking ganja. Wherever Homi looked, all she saw was hermits in their saffron robes. Her eyes kept searching for *him*, but she tired of her quest eventually, convinced that he was no longer pursuing her. She remembered trying to shove him out of the train. Perhaps she really was free now, perhaps she would never be confronted by her fate again.

When Chandra returned, Homi said, 'I've got the money you gave me, do you think I could use it to call Kolkata?'

'Come back to the mansion, Bibirani will let you use the phone.'

'Let's go, then.'

'Do you want to see the prayers here this evening, Homi?'

Homi told her that she did.

Chandra paid two rupees to have a priest put a dot of sandalwood paste and vermilion on her forehead. Her face glowed with pleasure afterwards. They headed back home, and on the way they met a middle-aged man. Chandra dipped her head and touched his feet reverently, and they had a short conversation.

'Do you know who that was, Homi? He's got miraculous powers, though you can't tell from his appearance. His chanting can cure the sick. When I was very young I fell ill with jaundice. He gave me some powder to swallow and said, I'm going to chant, just rub your hands together in this pot of water. Believe me, Homi, the water turned bright yellow. What a sight it was! Then he extracted yellow powder from my nose and ears.'

'And you were cured?'

Homi wasn't laughing.

'It took some time, but yes, I was.'

Back at the mansion, when Homi said she wanted to make a call, Bibirani told her to go right ahead.

It wasn't even 8 AM. Homi called her mother from a satin sofa in Bibirani's room. Mrs Banerjee exploded in anger as soon as she identified the voice at the other end.

'Come back right now, Khuku, wherever you are! How could you run away and leave your sick parents behind? Do you know I fainted on the staircase after having a tooth taken out? I had to go to the dentist all by myself. Just because I said I would go on holiday with Mita you decided you had to go on one too. Even Oli's been worrying about you.'

Hanging up, Homi called Yash at the office. But she had forgotten he didn't get in before nine, so she left a message for him with Bibirani's number. It was barely nine when he called back. Bibirani told Aina to fetch Homi.

'Where are you?' Yash's voice thick with worry.

'In Benaras.'

'How did you get there?'

'I just did.'

'Call Chetan, Homi. You've given him enough trouble already. I've nothing more to say to you. If you want to keep your job, email an application for leave right now.'

'Yash, I lost my bag and everything else three days ago. I haven't even had my SIM card deactivated.'

'Do you have any idea of the terrorist activity in Benaras these days? Who knows who's using your SIM. You're heading for big trouble, Homi. I really can't understand you.'

'I'll be back very soon, Yash.'

'Do you need money?'

'I'll let you know if I do,' Homi said after a pause. Yash scoffed.

'Which means you have some other plan.'

Homi hung up after taking Chetan's number from Yash.

'It's me, Homi.'

Chetan was infuriated.

'Forget it, Homi, I don't want to talk to you after what you did. Do you know the trouble you got me into? You jumped into a taxi and disappeared god knows where. I had to spend the whole night outside your boarding house. I kept calling your office to find out if you were there. Everyone knew you left with me, so they kept asking me questions. It was a totally ridiculous situation. Eventually I had to wake up the people in your boarding house. Now the women there, your mother, your colleagues, all of them are hounding me, asking where you are. We were about to start a relationship, Homi – thank god it didn't happen.'

—

Daniel arrived just as Homi and Chandra were about to leave for Dashashwamedh Ghat that evening. Chandra and Daniel exchanged glances, after which Daniel went off to see Bibirani.

He returned in a minute.

'May I accompany you?'

His pronunciation may not have been perfect, but his Hindi wasn't bad at all. Homi gazed at Chandra, who was dressed in a glamorous yellow sari with a flimsy sleeveless blouse, her hair piled high on her head.

There was only one reason that Chandra and Daniel had begun to like each other – fate. It was, as Mr Vaid had told Homi, a consequence. Daniel had come here all the way from Detroit, his visits to the mansion dictated by the fact that he took lessons in Indian classical music from Bibirani. Chandra was Bibirani's personal attendant, practically a member of her family. She was beautiful, lively, intelligent. She and Daniel were probably falling in love. Or maybe they merely liked each other. None of this was anything more than a particular set of circumstances. Lovers were nothing but two individuals who had become victims of the same circumstance.

There wasn't an inch of free space at Dashashwamedh Ghat. Those who wanted to watch the prayers from up close, which would be accompanied by lamps and devotional songs, had occupied all the spots on the staircase of the ghat since the afternoon. The raised walled terrace of the temple seemed to have been reserved for foreigners. Countless boats dotted the river, filled with people eager to catch a glimpse of the rituals. Six young men dressed in white silk dhotis and saffron silk shirts began the proceedings, holding large brass lamps which they moved in circular motions, ignoring the tongues of flame and extreme heat emanating from them. The singers were sitting in one corner of the ghat. Large floodlights came on, reducing the lamps to a dim glow.

Since it was impossible to see anything from where they were, Chandra led them to the adjoining ghat, which gave them a clear view. As she watched the proceedings, Homi felt India was a land of infants who would never grow up. As a child, she had used to mix talcum powder with water to make milk for her dolls. The people here seemed to be doing something similar, making pastes of sandalwood or vermilion. Then they daubed drops of the pastes on jasmine leaves and put flower petals in baskets, throwing them into the water as sacred objects. They also took triple-dips in the river, or spun around as they bobbed up and down, or poured milk into the river. Some wanted coins made with three kinds of metal to be rolled down the back of their heads into the water, others advised lighting a hundred and eight lamps, and yet others suggested holding fistfuls of leaves while wading in the river ...

A game, nothing but a game. Everyone in this immense land of India was engrossed in a game with their gods ...

Chandra and Daniel were sitting intimately together, his hand lightly touching her shoulder. Chandra was looking exquisite under the floodlight. Daniel was a handsome young man, but he was a pale shadow to her radiant, explosive beauty. They were trying to concentrate on the spectacle before them, but as soon as Homi moved away their attention shifted to each other. Had she not been there, Daniel would probably not have been able to broach the idea of accompanying Chandra to the ghat. But then Chandra was free to go anywhere she liked, since Bibirani did not control her movements. It was entirely possible that they regularly sat on the steps of an ancient ghat, gazing into each other's eyes with the eternally flowing water of the Ganga as witness. Perhaps Chandra felt Daniel would never leave her. Perhaps Daniel reflected on his extraordinary experiences in Benaras, with Chandra an indelible part of them, like these ghats – Dashashwamedh, Man Singh, Lalita, Manikarnika – like this temple, like the mansion in the lane where savouries were fried, like Bibirani's raga Shyamkosh, like the bulls and the hermits, like Hinduism. Maybe Daniel tried to understand Chandra the way he tried to make sense of this religion. How noble they both were, he might tell himself. Simple, too? And headily intoxicating.

Looking around her, Homi saw a boy praying all by himself on a terrace at the Man Singh Ghat. Why was he alone? Homi went up to him. Dressed in a dhoti hitched up to his knees, he had a single lamp in his right hand and a bell in his left. The fervent movement of his lips made listening unnecessary – Homi was convinced he was chanting passages from sacred texts. The movement of the boy's tiny fist made the flame leave a scar in the air. Homi felt her heart being sliced open the same way, by an invisible knife. No, the tears that flowed were not because she was alone, so completely alone, but because she was seeking not love, wisdom, or fulfilment – she sought to be exiled from the future, to be exiled from events. She wanted confinement, final and permanent, complete incarceration. Otherwise her loneliness would prove discordant and unsuccessful. Homi sat there gazing upon the water. Even time was cleansed, becoming pure, when passing over this river. It was so dark out there, she could not actually see the water. All she could make out was a strange pattern of differently sized moored boats. It was low tide now, with no current. The lights of the boats moving on the river were visible. They didn't stray far from the bank, merely going from one ghat to another.

Chandra shook Homi's shoulder.

'Bibirani called on Daniel's phone, Homi. Jahnavibai is very ill. And Parvatia's daughter ate rotten food at some temple and got such a bad attack of diarrhoea that she has to be taken to hospital. I'm going to spend the night at Jahnavibai's. You'd better go back with Daniel. Parvatia can't leave Jahnavibai till I get there, so I'm going there directly.'

Homi jumped to her feet.

'I'll come with you to Jahnavibai's, Chandra, I'll stay with you.'

'You mustn't,' Chandra warned her, 'Bibirani will be upset.'

'Why should she be upset?'

Homi saw tears glistening in Chandra's eyes.

'What is it, Chandra? Why are you crying?'

It was true, Chandra's sparkling beauty was eclipsed by an unfamiliar shroud of grief.

'I'll tell you later, Homi.'

'No, tell me now.'

The prayers had ended. Looking around for Daniel, that was what Homi discovered instead.

'Daniel's leaving, Homi. He'll be here for just a few days more. He'll go to Haridwar first, and then to Puri. He only has one more fortnight in Benaras. I didn't know. His visa is running out. It's expiring just as I'm falling in love with him.'

'You've made a mistake, Chandra,' Homi told her. 'You should have realised he would have to go back sooner or later.'

'How could I have? I don't want much, Homi, just for him to stay a little longer. Just one more month.'

Daniel held his phone out to Chandra. He had been standing next to them all the time.

'Bibirani's calling again.'

Chandra got a grip on herself.

'You'd better go back, Homi, I'll go to Jahnavibai.'

'Didn't I say I'd go with you, Chandra?'

Taking the phone, Homi told Bibirani she wanted to accompany Chandra to Jahnavibai's mansion. Bibirani did not object.

## AN ARDUOUS TASK
## UNDER AN EVIL STAR

Daniel was clearly not much older than Homi or Chandra. His face must have paled at Chandra's tears. It had been seven or eight months since he had arrived in Benaras – his second visit.

'Perhaps Daniel will be back again soon, who can tell.'

Chandra and Daniel walked side by side, while Homi was a few paces behind them. They climbed up the steps of the ghat to the road, and arrived at their lane. Soon Chandra was using the huge iron knocker to rap on the giant wooden door, which was secured by an oversized iron bolt. The relief work on the door had been eaten away by time. There were so many metal plates on it that it looked like the entrance to a jail. It was true that death had imprisoned someone in this mansion.

Daniel was about to turn away from the front door.

'Will you come back in two hours?' Chandra asked him.

'At this time of night?'

'How late will it be by then?' Chandra asked.

'Ten, maybe ten-thirty? We can slip out through the back and go to Manikarnika.'

'Is that possible?'

'Why not, there's a road leading to it.'

'I want to see if that's true.'

Daniel tucked away a stray lock of Chandra's hair from her forehead. Chandra clasped his hand for a moment before he left, before she and Homi entered Jahnavibai's mansion.

This mansion had a wall around it. Its owner-ship would pass to a missionary organisation after Jahnavibai's death. The paperwork was already done. The place would be converted to a residential Vedanta school, with young Brahmin boys moving in to study the Vedas in pure Devanagari script, dressed in short-ened dhotis, their heads shaved except for a tuft at the crown.

Chandra was unhappy at that moment, but she still exuded energy, a force that Homi would hesitate to call sexual desire. But it was true that she wanted Daniel. Perhaps her earlier hesitation had left her. No matter how permanent and immutable the distance between her and Daniel might seem, surely it could collapse for a few hours, a few days? Chandra clearly wasn't herself, as she paid no attention to the instructions Parvatia gave her before leaving.

Homi and Chandra entered Jahnavibai's room together. Starting with the curtains, everything was white. Maybe the owner couldn't stand anything colourful. What Homi saw even in the very dim light made her skin prickle. Was this woman really Jahnavibai, whose portrait she had seen in Bibirani's music room? How could someone once so beautiful look the way she did? Her gaunt body had merged with her bed, her face dented like a tin can, her brow hanging loose over her eyes. Jahnavibai was surviving on the medicinal concoctions made personally by the ayurvedic doctor Gangadhar Raut. Of late she had lost the desire to take her medicine, but she also lacked the strength to refuse.

Forgetting her own problems for a while, Chandra practically threw herself on Jahnavibai, wrapping her body around the old woman's.

'Does it hurt very much, Ma?'

There was no response from Jahnavibai, who only stared at Chandra and Homi.

'I'll be with you all the time from now on. I won't leave your side. I'll look after you myself. This is our guest Homi, she's here to see you. She's from Kolkata, a TV journalist, she's leaving in a couple of days.'

Chandra was talking without a pause. Jahnavibai looked to have fallen asleep, her chest rising and falling as though each breath was her last.

Homi went into the next room, which led to a roofless balcony overhanging the road. Its narrow stone railing, with carved lotuses, was no more than knee-high. There was a ghat close by, with smoke rising from it. Was it Manikarnika? Jahnavibai was close to the crematorium in more than one sense.

'What are you doing, Homi?'

Homi turned around to see Chandra arranging her lightly dishevelled clothes.

'Daniel's here, I heard him knocking. Do you want to eat anything? Sudha must have cooked, why don't you have dinner? Else Bibirani will be angry with me for letting you starve.'

'No Chandra, I don't want to eat. I've had a lot of heavy food already. I'm just going to have a glass of water and sit here on the balcony.'

Chandra hesitated.

'I'm going out for a bit, with Daniel. Don't tell Bibirani, all right?'

'I won't. I'm leaving tomorrow, Chandra.'

'So soon?'

'I think so.'

Chandra knew that everyone left when their time came. She went out, and Homi tried to spot her and Daniel from the balcony. She wasn't sure, since the lane outside was unlit, but she thought she heard the clinking of Chandra's bangles fading away to her left. After spending some time together, they might feel the urge to have sex. Then, they would return to the mansion. Nothing would get in their way tonight.

Homi sat there listening to the bells in the distance. The boats had vanished from the river. Then she heard what sounded like a glass fall to the floor in the next room. As Homi ran in, a faint but coarse voice said, 'You can do it. Yes, you.'

Was it Jahnavibai? Homi groped for the switch and the light came on. A face wracked by agony, such a painful way to live.

'Do you want something?' Homi asked.

'Death.'

Jahnavibai stirred impatiently.

Homi took her time before replying.

'You have to wait.'

'No, no longer.' A plaintive cry from an empty container.

'Release me. You can do it. That's what you're here for. I can see it.'

'What are you saying?'

'I was attached to life for as long as I could stand. Or else I'd have thrown myself into the river long ago. I'm helpless now, I don't know how to kill myself.'

Homi listened to Jahnavibai's reasoning, rooted to the spot in astonishment.

'You're not one of us. You've never seen me before. Why should you care whether I live or die? So much has been done for you. It's time for you to pay it back. Have mercy. Have mercy. A worse death awaits me otherwise – my body is full of sores, pus is gathering in them.'

Homi wondered why her own father was still alive. He should die, too, she thought. His body was covered in sores as well.

'Come. Come closer.'

Jahnavibai's eyes were boring into her. An irre-sistible desire to die had gathered in them. A pair of dangerously hypnotic eyes were pulling Homi, draw-ing her nearer. Homi felt herself approaching the woman. She was near her now, leaning over her.

'Strangle me, my child.'

The lines on Homi's palm held no love, no affec-tion, no regard, no attachment – was she going to prove them right or wrong, now? Was she pitying this woman? Lalit used to say she was too selfish, too in love with herself. Did that still hold true? Homi wrapped her hands around Jahnavibai's throat, pressing down with her fingers before giving a single hard squeeze. A muffled sound emerged from Jahnavibai's lips. Her mouth fell open, and her jaw went slack. Homi squeezed the woman's throat once more before loosening her hold. Jahnavibai's body fell back. Her eyes were popping out.

There was no sound anywhere now. Even the bells had fallen silent.

# AN IMAGINARY ACT OF SEX

Homi hadn't exactly wanted to escape, but nor had she wanted to wait for anything in particular, for Daniel and Chandra to return, for instance. She hadn't quite taken in what had happened a few moments ago, but then it wasn't as though she was entirely ignorant. She didn't know where to go at this hour of the night. But she also remembered she had two hundred rupees.

She climbed down the stairs and tried to ease the front door open. It opened easily, with barely a sound. Homi stepped into the lane and began to walk, not pausing, not even slowing down. The dogs barked at her but she continued on her way, paying no attention to them. There were patches of light and of darkness. The lane narrowed in some places and widened in others. She tried to tell herself at every moment that the main road was just a few steps away, she would be at the square in no time at all. She considered telling Bibirani that she had killed Jahnavibai at the woman's own request. Surely Bibirani would understand.

She kept walking, a succession of thoughts flashing through her mind. From one lane into another, and then yet another, all of them filthy, ugly, haunted. As dirty as hell. She realized gradually that she was wandering aimlessly, unable to get out of the lanes. Nor could she locate Bibirani's mansion. She was trapped in a labyrinth of lanes, returning to the same spot repeatedly. Now she began to run madly, trying to distinguish one lane from another, but without success. It began to feel like a black hole where she would choke to death. Panting and sweating, Homi finally found herself back outside Jahnavibai's mansion.

'Empress!'

The call penetrated deep into her heart. She turned around slowly, in no hurry whatsoever. There it was, that familiar face, those matted locks that demanded reverence, those eyes, possessed – flaming with love, with desire, with lust. The blue blanket slung over a shoulder. The freezing air. The stench.

'Empress!'

No, no one had ever called out to her this way.

'Come.'

Homi didn't spare a glance for anything else. She re-entered the mansion, climbing the stairs to the first floor. The hermit followed her. Her fate, whom she would no longer deprive of a union. Enough. They put their arms around each other. And at once Homi realised how hard, how cruel, how demonic his penis was. He threw off his loincloth, and she saw it throbbing, uncared for, unloved. And yet, this was her fate, which hadn't left her, which would not let her go, which would press her for love, which would demand sex.

She grew eager for it too, exposing her vulva. The man climbed on her, rubbing his lips on her breasts, her arms, her neck. Like a brazen lover he began to grind against the imaginary body of her imaginary life. And Homi held his enormous head between her imaginary hands – a heavy, immense head with matted hair.

She pressed the head to her breast with all the force she could summon.